THE
WINNING
OF
MISS LYNN RYAN

THE
WINNING
OF
MISS LYNN RYAN

ILENE COOPER
WITH ILLUSTRATIONS BY
SUSAN MAGURN

Morrow Junior Books
New York

For Dale from Gale

With thanks to Leslie Saul, director of the Insect Zoo at the
San Francisco Zoo

Text copyright © 1987 by Ilene Cooper

Illustrations copyright © 1987 by Susan Magurn

Printed in the United States of America.

1 2 3 4 5 6 7 8 9 10

Library of Congress Cataloging-in-Publication Data

Cooper, Ilene.
The winning of Miss Lynn Ryan.

Summary: No matter how hard she tries, Carrie
fails to impress her attractive, new fifth-grade
teacher who favors the more popular members of
the class and either ignores or criticizes Carrie and
her new friend Luke, the class nerd.
[1. Schools—Fiction. 2. Friendship—Fiction]
I. Magurn, Susan, ill. II. Title.
PZ7.C7856Wi 1987   [Fic]   87-15233
ISBN 0-688-07231-3

CHAPTER

CARRIE SAT DOWN AT HER DESK and watched as the black blot spread across the top of her composition. She had just been gone a minute, up to the wastebasket to throw away the crumpled balls of paper that seemed to grow on her desk. She must have forgotten to put the cap on her felt-tipped pen, and now her homework was ruined.

"Oh great," Carrie muttered, grabbing the pen. But before she could decide how to fix the paper, she heard Miss Ryan's high heels clicking down the aisle. They stopped next to her desk.

"Carrie Macphail," Miss Ryan began ominously, "I told the class I wanted just your compositions out."

Guiltily, Carrie looked up. "This is it," she started in a rush. "It's about my dog Taffy and how I taught him to . . ."

Miss Ryan sighed. "You know neatness counts, Carrie. Fifth-graders should pay attention to their work. I don't think you want to hand this in. Do you?" she asked pointedly.

"I guess not. I'll do it over." Carrie watched Miss Ryan shake her head as she continued down the aisle picking up papers. Why me? Carrie wondered as she took out another sheet of notebook paper and began laboriously writing her name, the date and her room number in the corner. She glanced up and saw Beth Stone looking at her with pity.

This would never happen to Beth, Carrie thought, too glum to acknowledge her best friend's sympathetic smile. As usual, Beth looked positively angelic with her bouncy blond curls, big blue eyes and squeaky clean clothes. Even her jeans looked as if they'd just been pressed.

Carrie was a different story and she knew it. No matter how neatly dressed she was when she left her room, it wasn't five minutes before a juice stain appeared on her sweater or there'd be a tear in her blouse. Carrie's fine brown hair escaped from her long braid within seconds of having a rubber band choked around it. And what didn't get messy just seemed to disappear—socks, barrettes, library books, schoolwork, Taffy's leash and her lunch money.

"She has her feet on the ground," parents and

teachers would say approvingly about Beth. When it came to Carrie it was more likely to be: "She has her head in the clouds." Carrie knew that meant she daydreamed too much and didn't pay attention, but secretly she thought poking around in the sky sounded a lot more interesting than just plodding along on the sidewalk.

"Earth to Carrie," Beth would say when Carrie was walking alongside her but thinking about something else.

"I heard you," Carrie always answered with irritation, but she hardly ever knew what Beth had been saying. Usually, they started laughing about it. That was one of the best things about Beth as far as Carrie was concerned. She hated arguments and she definitely preferred laughing to fighting.

Being a daydreamer and a little careless were just things Carrie accepted about herself, like the sprinkle of freckles on the bridge of her nose. They never really bothered her—not until she had gone into Miss Ryan's room, anyway.

"Since I'm new to Kennedy Middle School, I'd like to take some time to introduce myself," Miss Ryan had said when school began, just a month ago.

"My name is Lynn Ryan and I grew up in New York, but I went to college in Chicago. I decided I liked it here and wanted to stay in the area. Last year I taught in Oak Ridge and now I'm looking forward to working and living here in Forest Glen."

Carrie couldn't keep her eyes off Miss Ryan that first day in class. She was so different from any other teacher Carrie had ever had. It wasn't just that she was pretty, even though she was. And it wasn't that she had great-looking clothes, even though she did. There was something about the way Miss Ryan acted—as though she knew everyone would think she was terrific—that attracted Carrie like steel to a magnet.

At recess that first day, some of the girls clustered together and started talking about Miss Ryan.

"She's so young," Wendy Chu said. "I bet she's really going to be fun."

"I'm just glad we have a woman teacher," Beth put in. "We were stuck with Mr. Grady for two years."

"He's not here this year, is he?" Michelle Mitchell asked.

Carrie giggled. "No, that old get-up-and-go he was always talking about finally got up and left."

Mr. Grady had also doubled as the gym teacher and sometimes it seemed as if he was coaching fourth grade instead of teaching it.

"We're winners!" he'd shout. "We're going to get

those arithmetic books out and show 'em who's boss, right, team?"

Despite Mr. Grady's hearty urgings, Carrie never quite figured out how to show her math book she was boss. In fact, if her math book knew anything, it was that Carrie still needed her fingers to add and subtract. Carrie didn't think she'd ever be able to do arithmetic without at least one hand counting under the desk.

As the first month of school passed, Carrie tried to figure out what made Miss Ryan so special. For one thing, she wasn't afraid of her class the way some new teachers were—but she wasn't a bully either. Carrie was also surprised at the way Miss Ryan, right from the first, seemed able to pick out the kids who were most popular and pay special attention to them. Everybody liked Randy Jackson because he was so funny and nice. By the second day of the semester, Miss Ryan had picked him to be the monitor whenever she was out of the room.

Carrie hadn't been chosen for any classroom jobs and she was waiting impatiently for that to change. She couldn't put it into words, but there was something about Miss Ryan that made Carrie wish the teacher would notice her, really notice her. It would be wonderful if Miss Ryan would single her out for some special attention.

"Carrie?"

Carrie looked up from her composition hopefully.

"You aren't redoing your theme now, are you?" Miss Ryan asked with a frown.

"Well . . ."

"Carrie, we don't start our sentences with a 'well' unless we're talking about a hole in the ground."

"I wanted to get my composition back to you right away," Carrie explained.

"We're doing history now. Take out your book and open it to page twenty-three as the rest of the class has already done. Rewrite your paper at home, not on our time."

Carrie nodded and reached for her history book.

So much for special attention.

MOST OF THE STUDENTS had cleared out for the day, but Carrie hung around the back of the room hoping that Miss Ryan might have some time to answer a question about their science projects, which were due in a few weeks. She knew Miss Ryan liked her students to show an interest in their assignments— well, some of her students anyway. At the moment, Miss Ryan was at her desk with Luke Olson and she didn't look a bit happy about it.

Carrie could understand why. Luke wasn't very popular with the fifth grade. He wore short-sleeve shirts like the kind you saw on grown men, and he had a nasty habit of picking his many scabs.

But the thing that really set Luke Olson apart was his great love of bugs. He always had a book about spiders or beetles with him, and about the only time he spoke up in class was when there was a discussion of insects under way. Since that didn't happen often, Luke spent a lot of his time gazing out the window.

Most of the kids laughed at Luke behind his back, but Freddy Butler was the meanest by far. Luke sat two seats behind Freddy, making it easy for Freddy to stick out his foot and trip Luke almost every time he walked by. The odd thing was, Luke didn't seem to care about the laughing or the tripping. He ignored them all, even Freddy.

"Carrie, I've been waiting outside for you forever." Beth tugged impatiently on Carrie's sleeve.

Carrie gave a final glance in Miss Ryan's direction, but she and Luke were still deep in conversation. "Okay," Carrie agreed, "let's go home." She gathered her books off the science table and slowly followed Beth into the schoolyard.

A group of fifth- and sixth-grade girls, including Wendy and Michelle, were standing on the edge of the playfield. They were watching Randy and some of the other boys who were kicking a soccer ball around.

"Oh, look, a game," Beth said. "Let's stick around for a while."

"Do we have to?" Carrie griped. "It's so boring."

"But everyone else is staying," Beth said, her eyes

searching the field for Randy.

"Like my mother says, if everyone jumped into Lake Michigan, would you?"

Beth ignored that. "I'm staying," she said, walking over to the girls.

Carrie's bad mood deepened, but she joined the circle.

"I was thinking," Wendy said, "if the boys get up a soccer team, maybe we could be cheerleaders."

"Beth could be Randy's personal cheerleader," Michelle said slyly.

Beth took a swipe at Michelle, but she didn't deny her words.

"Why should we watch the boys play?" Carrie asked. "We could play ourselves if we wanted to."

"But you're not good at soccer. Or any sports," Michelle reminded her.

"I said if we wanted to. What I meant was, we could be doing something, not just standing around here."

"My mother says I either have to be in the schoolyard or at home," Michelle answered primly.

"I don't mind standing here," Beth said, as the soccer ball rolled toward her feet with Randy Jackson right behind it.

"Thanks," he called as Beth gave the ball a little kick in his direction. A shy smile came to Beth's face.

The game went on for a few more minutes, but when Randy said he had to leave for the dentist, most of the girls on the sidelines began to drift away too. Wendy, Michelle, Carrie and Beth headed for the iron gates that led to the street.

"Has anybody picked a topic for their science projects yet?" Beth asked.

"I have," Wendy answered. "I'm going to do something with sound waves."

Michelle flipped her long dark hair over one shoulder. "My mother's going to help me decide tonight." Michelle's mother was always helping her do something.

Carrie didn't know what she was going to do yet. Miss Ryan had told the class, "Pick some aspect of science that interests you and do something creative to explain it. Charts, dioramas, you know what I mean. The ones with the best potential may be expanded into science fair projects."

Carrie knew that the class would only be allowed a couple of entries into the school science fair and she doubted that her project would be one of them. She wasn't much better in science than she was in math. Still, she was going to give it her best. This was the first big assignment Miss Ryan had given the class and Carrie felt it was a chance to show her teacher what she could do.

With a wave, Carrie and Beth left the schoolyard

and turned toward their houses.

"I think I'm going to identify leaves for my science project," Beth said, picking up a maple leaf swirled with red, orange and green.

"That's kind of easy, isn't it?"

"I suppose so," Beth agreed. "But Miss Ryan didn't say the project had to be complicated, just something we're interested in."

"Lots of kids are going to be interested in leaves, I bet," Carrie said knowingly.

Beth giggled. "You're right. Maybe I'll explain how leaves change color. That way mine will be different from all the other leaf posters."

Trust Beth to figure out a good project, Carrie thought. If only she had had the chance to talk to Miss Ryan this afternoon, maybe she would have come up with something by now. Carrie's thoughts flitted back to the classroom; then she formed the question that had been bothering her for a while now. "Beth, do you think I'm like Luke Olson?"

Beth looked at her as though she were joking. "Luke the Puke? Oh, right, you're just like him. You pick your scabs and you're crazy about insects. You two could be twins."

Carrie gave Beth a small smile. She had never said much to Beth about getting in Miss Ryan's good graces. It had seemed too personal to talk about. But maybe it would be good to get her opinion—Beth was her best friend and she wouldn't make fun of her. At least Carrie hoped she wouldn't.

"Well, maybe Luke and I do have something in common," she said carefully. "Miss Ryan doesn't like either of us."

Beth had been stopping every few steps to pick up the best leaves for her project. Now she halted in surprise. "Miss Ryan doesn't like you? I never noticed that. I mean, she isn't real nice to you like she is to Wendy or Randy . . ."

"Or you," Carrie finished for her.

"Or me," Beth slowly agreed, "but she doesn't yell at you or anything."

"She doesn't yell at anybody."

"I guess not." Beth resumed walking with a thoughtful look on her face. "She doesn't even yell at Luke and he can be a real pain."

"But when she tells you to do something in a certain way, you wind up feeling like a worm."

Beth considered this. "She talks to almost everyone like that once in a while."

"Not to you," Carrie answered, envy creeping into her voice.

Beth looked uncomfortable. "Carrie, Miss Ryan likes you fine. Don't worry about it."

"Yeah, you're probably right." There wasn't much

else to say. It's the weekend, she told herself. Forget about school.

The five-block walk to their subdivision never seemed very long. Talking always made it go faster and today was no exception. The girls stopped as they usually did in front of Beth's comfortable white brick house. "Want to come in?" Beth asked. "Maybe Jane made some scones."

Jane was the Stones' *au pair* girl from England. As far as Carrie could tell, *au pair* was a fancy French phrase that just meant baby-sitter. Jane had come to Forest Glen for a year and in exchange for her room and board she took care of Beth's little brother Sam and did some light housekeeping. In her spare time, Jane took lessons at the Art Institute in downtown Chicago.

"Is Jane home?" Carrie asked. "I thought she had classes today."

"No, they were canceled."

"Too bad. Jane hates to miss those art classes."

"If you ask me, she's wasting her money if they keep on teaching her to do those big blobby paintings," Beth said.

"I don't know. I think they're kind of neat."

"You just think everything Jane does is neat."

Jane was sometimes a sore point between the girls. Although they both liked her, she was a little too punk for Beth. Jane didn't have a shaved head or anything, but there was a maroon streak in her short brown hair that Carrie thought was great and Beth thought was awful.

"Not everything, but I do like her pictures."

"And her clothes," Beth prompted.

"They're cool."

Beth made a face. "Black turtleneck, black skirt and those safety pins she wears—weird."

"Beth, she only keeps the pins there for changing Sam's diapers."

"Well, who knows. One day she might put them through her ears or something."

Carrie giggled. "C'mon, Beth. At least we can both agree that Jane's a great baker."

Baking wasn't part of Jane's job but she enjoyed it and regularly whipped up goodies. Her specialties were shortbread and biscuit-like scones made to be eaten with thick butter and strawberry jam. Carrie just loved them. Most afternoons, even when she knew she should get home, she couldn't resist stopping at Beth's.

As soon as Beth flung open the door, Carrie started sniffing. Instead of the heavenly scent of fresh-baked scones, however, all Carrie could smell were Sam's wet diapers waiting in a bag by the door to go to the diaper service.

"Hello there." Jane came into the front hall holding the squirmy Sam. "Give us a rest, will you, luv?" she said, thrusting Sam into Beth's arms and collapsing on the stairs. Sometimes it seemed to Carrie that Jane, with her English accent and streaked hair, came from another planet, instead of another country.

"Sure," Beth said, giving Sam a kiss on his cheek. If Beth looked like an angel, Sam was a fat blond cherub.

"Did you have a nice day?" Jane asked, stifling a yawn.

"It was fine," Beth answered absently while Carrie nodded shyly in agreement. "Jane, I think he's wet."

"Again? I don't know where it all comes from."

"I'll change him," Beth said.

"Oh, would you? That would be lovely."

There were obviously no scones and since Carrie didn't want to stay around for the icky job of changing diapers, she decided this would be a good time to make her exit.

"I guess I'll go home, Beth."

Beth looked distracted as Sam started to fuss. "Okay, I'll talk to you later," she said, inching her way around Jane so she could climb the stairway to Sam's room.

Jane looked at Carrie with concern. "Sorry, hope I didn't spoil some plans."

"Oh no, I just stopped in because I thought there might be . . ." Carrie suddenly realized how rude she might sound.

"Scones or shortbread?" Jane laughed.

"Scones."

"Maybe tomorrow, Carrie." Jane pulled herself up off the steps and walked Carrie to the door.

"They're very good," Carrie said, embarrassed.

"I'm glad you like them, luv. I do, too. They remind me of home."

Carrie thought about Jane's words as she walked down the block to her own house. How must it feel to be in a foreign country? And live in someone's basement? The paneled room at the Stones' was fixed up nicely and it had its own TV and bathroom, but still . . . For her part, Carrie couldn't imagine what it would be like to have an outsider living in her house all the time. She remembered back to some of the fights she had with her parents. She wouldn't have liked to have anyone overhearing them.

The idea of scones had set Carrie's stomach rumbling. It was possible that her dad had baked something. Once in a while he did, though he wasn't the greatest cook in the world. Ever since she was little, Mr. Macphail had taught at the university, going to his office in the English department early in the morning and coming home by two o'clock. So afternoons were their special times together until Mrs.

Macphail came home from work.

Carrie could hear Taffy barking as soon as she came up the walk. "Hi, Taf." Carrie waved at the golden cocker spaniel, who stood quivering against the picture window. As soon as she opened the door, Taffy threw himself at Carrie with total abandon.

"Taffy, are you protecting us from another dangerous burglar?" Mr. Macphail called from the den.

Carrie giggled. Her father was always joking around. About 75 percent of the time he was funny. The rest of the time his jokes were just dumb. She wandered into the den where her father, dressed in sweats, sat on the sofa in his usual pose: glasses pushed on top of his balding head, huge feet encased in running shoes draped over the coffee table and cookie crumbs dotting his beard. He was in the process of marking his students' papers, which were in little piles all around him.

" 'Carry on. Love is coming,' " her dad sang from an old song from the sixties as she came over to give him a kiss. He was always fooling around with her name. Sometimes it was, "Carry me back to old Virginie." She didn't mind the singing, but she hated it when he called her Care Bear.

Stepping over the stack of papers that were graded A, Carrie pecked her dad on the cheek and grabbed two Oreos from his side table. The Chicago Cubs game blared in the background.

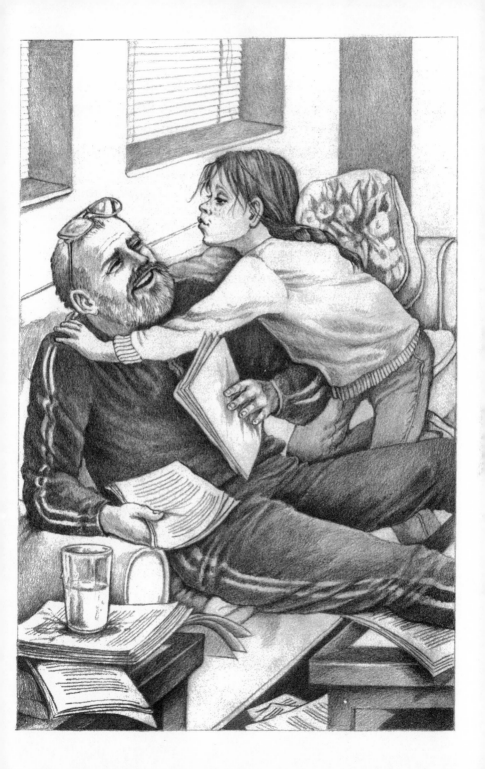

"Turn off the TV and talk to me, Car."

"Are they losing?" she asked idly as she went over to the television and lowered the sound.

"Of course. Do you think I'd take time out to chat if the Cubs were ahead?"

Carrie made a face. "Daddy, it's a good thing I don't take you seriously."

Mr. Macphail shook his head. " 'A prophet is without honor in his own home.' "

"What does that mean?" Carrie asked as she moved some papers and sat on the floor.

"It means you don't take me seriously."

Carrie rolled her eyes.

"How was school?" he asked while he sorted through his tests.

"Oh, okay," Carrie answered, picking at the knot in her sneakers.

Looking up, Mr. Macphail said quietly, "Doesn't sound all that okay."

"No, it was. I have to think of a science project."

Mr. Macphail went back to his grading. "Well, that's your mom's area." Mrs. Macphail worked at the university hospital. She did something with blood. The sight of blood made Carrie sick to her stomach, so she tried to avoid discussing her mother's job.

"You went to college. You must have learned something about science."

"Carrie, you are looking at a man who almost flunked out of Harper College because he didn't know his Jupiter from his Saturn in astronomy class."

"I've got to come up with something really good." Carrie's voice was tinged with desperation.

"Why don't you show how a computer works?" her father suggested, eyes down, his red pen checking off answers.

"How does a computer work?"

"We'll ask your mother."

"I have to do my English composition over," Carrie said softly.

"How come?" he asked, his eyes now on her face.

"I got some ink on it."

"Carrie wasn't being careful, huh?"

Even though Carrie knew he was kidding, she started to get mad. "It was just an accident."

Mr. Macphail's smile faded. He grabbed his glass of milk from a pile of tests on the side table. "Hey, it could happen to anyone."

"Oh sure."

"Honestly, Car." Then he looked down at the papers. The top test sported a big round wet stain. He held it up toward Carrie. The smile crept back up his lips. "What did I tell you? Anyone."

BY THE TIME Mrs. Macphail arrived home from work, Carrie and her father were putting dinner on the table.

"Kentucky Fried Chicken again?" Mrs. Macphail moaned as she slumped down on one of the wooden kitchen chairs. Carrie continued setting out paper plates and napkins. Let Daddy handle this one, she thought. I told him he should have bought Chinese.

"Now, Ann," her father said, patting Mrs. Macphail's short sandy-colored hair. "You know fried chicken is your favorite."

"We have salad, too," Carrie put in. "I made it."

Her mother turned toward her with smiling gray eyes, just the same color as Carrie's. "Well, at least someone here is worried about our nutrition."

Nutrition. That meant eating properly, Carrie

knew. The word rang a bell in her head. Maybe nutrition would make a good science project. She turned toward her mother, who was washing her hands at the sink. "Mom, I have to do a science project. Do you think nutrition is a good subject?"

Mrs. Macphail efficiently wiped her hands and threw away the paper towel. "It's a big subject, Carrie. Maybe you could pick just one part of it."

"Like what?" Carrie asked as she slipped into the chair next to her father's. He was already helping himself to a juicy chicken breast.

"Maybe you could write about the importance of breakfast," Mr. Macphail said slyly. He knew Carrie hated breakfast with a passion. She particularly hated eggs. In all their forms—squishy scrambled, oozing over easy or rubbery hard-boiled—they could be summed up in one word: *yucky*. Once she had tried to teach Taffy how to balance an egg on his nose. The bad part was that Taffy couldn't do it. The good part was that it had used up a week's supply of eggs.

"Why don't you take just one nutritious food?" suggested Mrs. Macphail, waving a drumstick. "That might be the easiest."

Carrie considered this. One food. That didn't sound too hard. She would find out all she could about it and then make a big chart. "What's a real nutritious food?" she asked.

"Fried chicken," answered her father as he helped himself to another piece.

"He's kidding," Mrs. Macphail said, shaking her head at him. "I believe soybeans are the most nutritious food."

Carrie made a face. "Soybeans? Bor-ing."

Her mother shrugged. "What do you consider to be an interesting food?"

"Oreos."

"Interesting *and* nutritious."

Carrie thought for a minute. Whenever she absolutely refused to eat something at dinner, her mother let her have a peanut butter sandwich, so that had to be pretty healthy. "Peanut butter?" she ventured.

"Not a bad choice, Carrie," her father said, picking a few crumbs out of his beard. "Except I'd stick with just the peanut if I were you. You start talking about peanut butter and pretty soon you have to start talking about jelly. Definitely not nutritious."

"Okay, the peanut." Carrie stared dreamily out the kitchen window. She could see it all now. A chart wouldn't be enough to impress Miss Ryan. Maybe she could make some kind of video. That was it, a video starring that peanut guy with a top hat and cane. The one on the peanut jars. What was his name? Of course. How silly, it was Mr. Peanut. All right, Mr. Peanut could tell all the great things about peanuts in this video. She would just have to find out what some of them were. Suddenly her glorious Technicolor video ground to a halt. Did she just hear her mother say the name Luke Olson?

". . . and Candy said they can stay over there."

Carrie looked at her suspiciously. "Who's Candy?"

"Weren't you paying attention?" Mrs. Macphail asked. "Candy Olson, Luke's mother."

"What about her?"

"As I was saying, we decided to share a baby-sitter when your dad and I go out with Mrs. Olson tomorrow. You'll go to Luke's house and we'll pick you up when our dinner is over."

Carrie looked at her mother, aghast. What was this, some kind of a weird joke? She vaguely remembered that her mother knew Mrs. Olson from the hospital, but they weren't friends. Now, all of a sudden, they were going out to dinner and she was going to share a baby-sitter with Luke? No way. "Forget it, Mom."

"Forget what?" her mother asked sharply.

"I wouldn't be caught dead with Luke. And I've told you about a million times, I don't need a baby-sitter."

"Come on, Carrie. We wouldn't want anyone to carry you away," Mr. Macphail said, trying to lighten the mood.

Carrie thought quickly. She knew she would lose

on the baby-sitter issue, but maybe there was still a chance she wouldn't have to go over to Luke's. "All right, get me a baby-sitter. Get me Mrs. Brady or Tina Arnold."

"I couldn't get anyone, Carrie," Mrs. Macphail replied. "And when I told Candy, she said Luke's older sister wouldn't mind staying with both of you as long as it was at their house."

Luke's sister the baby-sitter? This was getting more horrible by the second. "But, Mom, you don't understand. Luke is really a creep. All the kids would laugh if they found out I went over there."

"Carrie Ann Macphail," her father broke in angrily, "I don't like to hear you calling other children names."

Tears came to Carrie's eyes. Her father almost never yelled at her, but she didn't feel like backing down. Her father's tone of voice made her even madder.

"I'm not going," Carrie said defiantly.

"I'm afraid you are," Mrs. Macphail insisted. "This is a hospital party. Candy works at the hospital and this is the most reasonable solution."

"Not for me it isn't," Carrie shouted, throwing down her napkin. She took off toward her room with Taffy snapping at her heels. Then, slamming the door, she took Taffy in bed with her and pulled up

to her chin the red and white quilt her grand-mother had made.

"If they think I'm spending one minute at Luke the Puke Olson's house, they're crazy," she told Taffy.

Taffy looked at her with understanding brown eyes and Carrie gave him a big hug. In her heart, however, she knew that she would probably wind up going to the Olsons'. That was one of the problems with being an only child: it was always two against one. Well, if the worst happened, she was going to make Luke swear he'd never, ever mention she was in his house. If he even whispered she had put one toe in his buggy old house, she was going to do something awful to him. Carrie had a fine imagination, but she couldn't quite figure out what that something was. After all, he was already Luke Olson. What could be worse than that?

CHAPTER

4

CARRIE GRABBED THE HALL TELEPHONE on the first
ring. Her parents were still asleep—at least, she
thought they were—and she didn't want to wake
them. She wasn't in the mood to see them right
now. She hadn't seen them since dinner.

Carrie had spent the evening reading a really good
book called *Mrs. Frisby and the Rats of NIMH*.
When she had heard her parents going out for a
walk, she sneaked into the bathroom, got ready for
bed and was back in her room before they returned.

For some kids, spending time by themselves was
a punishment, but Carrie enjoyed being alone in
her cozy bedroom. It was decorated just the way she
liked it, with all her stuffed animals sitting on a
shelf and posters of her favorite rock stars on the
walls. There was plenty to read, an emergency bag

of potato chips in her underwear drawer and even a transistor radio if she got tired of reading. With Taffy sleeping on the floor or scampering around in her bed, it was the perfect place to hide out. Which was probably why her parents punished her by taking away her television privileges instead of sending her to her room.

"Hello," she whispered cautiously into the telephone.

"What are you whispering for?" asked Beth.

"I don't want to wake my parents," she answered, skirting the real issue. "What's up?"

"Want to go to the mall this morning? My mom's got an appointment with the eye doctor, so she can drive us over and pick us up when she's done."

Carrie hesitated. It sounded good to her, but she wasn't sure if her mother would let her. She might still be mad. On the other hand, her evening was already going to be ruined. Why shouldn't she have some fun during the day? "Sure, I can go," Carrie decided.

"Okay, great," Beth said happily. "We'll pick you up in about an hour."

The phone was hardly out of her hand when Carrie heard her mother say simply, "Go where?"

Carrie whirled around and saw her mother in her old chenille bathrobe, rubbing her eyes. "Beth wants me to go to the mall. Her mother's driving."

"Do you think you should be allowed to go after that little performance you put on last night?"

"It wasn't a performance. I really don't want to go to Luke's house."

Mrs. Macphail laughed in spite of herself. "I gathered that. And what's your opinion about that subject today?"

"I don't have a choice, do I?" Carrie muttered, not meeting her mother's gaze.

"No." Mrs. Macphail sighed.

"Then I guess I'll go to Luke's."

"Then I guess you can go to the mall." Her mother hesitated. "I'm sorry you're not happy about the arrangements I made, Carrie, but sometimes things just have to be a certain way."

Carrie looked at her mother guiltily. Usually, they got along pretty well and she didn't like to see her mother upset. "I know. It's okay. Thanks for letting me go to the mall."

"You're welcome."

Carrie was glad to see her mother brighten, but inside she was still mad about having to spend the evening with Luke.

Carrie dressed quickly in her best jeans and a denim work shirt her grandmother had embroidered with flowers and butterflies. After breakfast—a sip of orange juice—and a quick walk around the block with Taffy, she went back outside just in time to see the Stones' car making its way slowly down the street. Jerkily, it pulled up to her house and shuddered a little after it stopped.

"Hi, Carrie. Get in," Beth said, pushing over to make room in the front seat.

"Hi, Beth. Good morning, Mrs. Stone."

"Mmmh," Beth's mother answered without taking her eyes off the road. Mrs. Stone hated to drive and she really wasn't very good at it. She stomped on the brake a good deal and always made little gasping sounds when a car zoomed by her. She preferred her passengers to be quiet so she could concentrate. The silence and her shaky driving made the ten-minute ride to the mall seem a lot longer.

"Well, here we are," Mrs. Stone said with obvious relief when she pulled in front of the mall's main entrance. She pushed her hand through her thick blond hair. "I'll meet you here in an hour and a half. Right here. Do you know where we are?"

Beth looked at her with pity. "Of course."

"Right. So then I'll meet you back on this spot at twelve-thirty. Don't keep me waiting."

The girls scrambled out of the car and watched Mrs. Stone inch her way into traffic like a determined little ant.

Carrie shook her head. "If she hates driving so much, why does she do it?"

"She thinks it makes her brave."

"What do you think?"

"I think it makes her brave. A brave bad driver. Let's go inside."

Carrie liked the shopping mall. She never had enough money to buy anything important, but she enjoyed the hustle and bustle. She also had a keen interest in watching the other shoppers—for instance, that couple standing in front of the jewelry store window. They were engaged, Carrie decided. Or maybe they were about to get engaged and were looking for diamond rings. Maybe he was just a poor college student and couldn't afford to buy her the ring she liked.

"Earth to Carrie," Beth said, waving a hand in front of her friend's face. "Who is it now?"

"That couple over there." Carrie gestured. "They're having a fight about diamond rings."

Beth fell in with the story immediately. "He's rich and she's poor?"

"Nope, the opposite. She wants a big two-carat ring and he can only afford a little dinky diamond."

The girls were already walking toward the jewelry store to get a better look at the couple, but they disappeared into the crowd.

"Darn," Carrie said. "There they go."

Beth was staring dreamily into the jewelry store window.

"Thinking about which ring you'd like Randy to give you?" Carrie teased.

Beth flushed. "You're the one who's always daydreaming about stuff, not me," she said crossly. "Let's just go to Disc City and see if we can find something for Wendy's birthday."

After they picked up the new Springsteen album, Beth led the way to Pretty Ears to check out some earrings.

As far as Carrie was concerned, pierced ears fell in the same category as blood and eggs—things to be avoided. She stood by, bored, while Beth held up little hearts to her ears, then tiny ducks.

"Ducks in your ears?" Carrie made a face.

"All the sixth-grade girls are wearing little animal earrings."

"Well, I like the hearts better."

In the end, Beth didn't buy either pair and the girls decided to have Cokes in the middle of the mall where all the food stalls were. You could get everything there, from moo shu pork to McDonald's.

"So what are you doing tonight?" Beth asked idly as she stirred the leftover ice in her drink with a straw.

Carrie hesitated. She wanted to tell Beth about going to Luke's house, but the words just wouldn't come out. She took another sip of her Coke and shrugged.

"We're going to my grandmother's for dinner," Beth complained. "Then we have to go to her piano recital."

Carrie started laughing and almost spit out her drink. "I thought only kids had piano recitals."

"So did I," Beth said with disgust. "But Grandma never had a chance to take piano when she was little and now my mother says we all have to be supportive."

"What's she playing?" Carrie asked as she pictured Beth's silver-haired dumpling of a grandmother banging on the ivories.

" 'The Spinning Song.' "

This made both Carrie and Beth laugh so hard that Carrie started choking and a lady shopper came up and asked them if they were all right. They nodded and said thank you, but the second she left, they began laughing all over again.

Finally Beth wiped her eyes. "Carrie, I think I want to get those little duck earrings. Let's go back to Pretty Ears."

Carrie groaned. "It's all the way on the other side of the mall."

"It won't take long."

"But I wanted to go to the bookstore."

"You always want to go to the bookstore."

Carrie started to protest, but Beth just waved her down. "All right, I'll meet you there in twenty minutes."

"Fine," Carrie said happily. After Beth walked away, Carrie headed toward the bookstore, her eyes, as usual, scanning the crowd. Suddenly she felt like a cartoon character who had just received a jolt of electricity. Even the hair on the back of her neck prickled. There, walking through the mall, just like a regular person, was Miss Ryan!

Of course, it had occurred to Carrie that her teacher probably did all the things most people did—go shopping, return library books, do her laundry. But she never thought she might actually see Miss Ryan in one of those pursuits.

Carrie waited until Miss Ryan stopped in front of the video store window. Then when she began moving again, Carrie followed at a distance. As Miss Ryan strolled along, Carrie had plenty of opportunity to observe her. She noticed the way Miss Ryan's dark hair fell around her shoulders. Naturally curly, Carrie thought enviously. She carefully checked out the teacher's outfit—pretty nice. Miss Ryan was wearing jeans and a bright red sweater decorated with tiny white lambs. A blue work shirt that looked a lot like Carrie's was peeking out from underneath the sweater. Miss Ryan was like someone in a television commercial, Carrie decided, or maybe a model in a magazine. Carrie absently patted her own hair, which she hadn't bothered to braid. She wondered if her mother would let her get a perm.

Keeping a decent interval between them, Carrie followed Miss Ryan into the Neiman-Marcus department store. In a moment, they passed through Children's Clothes and moved into Lingerie. Carrie turned to her left and saw a counter full of bras—big ones. Quickly, she averted her eyes. Bras were not something Carrie had to worry about at the moment, and she couldn't ever imagine filling any that large.

It seemed for a second that Carrie had lost sight of Miss Ryan, but then she spotted her over by a display of slips. Carrie watched for a moment as Miss Ryan picked up first a pink slip and then a blue one. Briefly, she touched the lace on the bottom of the blue slip and suddenly a rush of embarrassment shot through Carrie. Buying underwear was pretty personal, she thought. You really didn't have the right to watch people buy their underwear, no matter how much you liked them. Slowly she backed out of the Lingerie department and wandered back to Children's Clothes.

A white sweater embroidered with pink pigs caught Carrie's eye. It was almost like Miss Ryan's. She picked it up and held it against her, but then she saw the price tag dangling from the cuff of the sleeve. Eighty-five dollars for a sweater? Carrie knew there was no way her parents would pay that. She seriously doubted if they'd pay that for her whole wardrobe. She hurriedly put down the sweater, moved toward the exit and almost bumped into Miss Ryan.

"Uh, hi, Miss Ryan," Carrie said guiltily. Come on, Carrie told herself, she can't know you were following her.

Miss Ryan looked down absently. For a second, a puzzled little frown played around her eyes, then it cleared. "Oh, hello, Carrie." She gave Carrie a quick smile and walked away.

Carrie stood still for a moment, then headed on toward the glass doors. She looked at her watch. She was already five minutes late. Beth was going to kill her.

When Carrie arrived panting at the bookstore, she found Beth in a corner looking through paperback romances.

"Sorry," Carrie said.

"We'd better meet my mother. It's twelve-thirty

now." Beth carefully placed *Swept Away by Love* on the revolving rack. "What took you so long?"

Carrie shrugged. "Just looking at stuff."

"Did you find anything interesting?"

"Yeah," Carrie said softly.

"Well, you can tell me about it in the car."

Carrie nodded but didn't say anything. She shoved her hands in her jacket pockets, relieved she was going home.

Later that afternoon, Carrie rode her bike over to the library and checked out three books on peanuts. She took them up to her room and started to read one with a nice fat peanut on the cover, but before she got too far into it, she fell asleep. It was near dusk when her mother poked her head in the doorway and whispered, "Carrie, wake up."

As soon as she opened her eyes, Carrie knew that something bad was about to happen, but she couldn't remember what. Then it hit her. She was on her way to Luke Olson's house.

Carrie was never in the best mood when she got up and this thought did nothing to cheer her. She made her way to the bathroom and splashed some cool water on her face. When her eyes opened a little, she caught sight of herself in the mirror. Her hair was all stringy and tangled and there was a big crease down the side of her cheek. Good, she thought. The way she looked pleased her. It seemed entirely fitting she should look like this when she was going to Luke's.

CHAPTER

5

"WE'LL BE AT THE AMBER INN," Mrs. Macphail informed Carrie as they drove along. Unlike Mrs. Stone, Carrie's mother enjoyed driving and often took the wheel instead of her husband. Mr. Macphail sat next to his wife, marking his students' test papers. He was always behind with his grading, so he used any and every opportunity to catch up.

"How long do you think this dinner you're going to will last?" Carrie asked glumly.

"Well, it's in honor of the hospital director, who's retiring, so there'll be some speeches after the meal."

"Boring speeches," Mr. Macphail put in, "but at least I can grade papers while they're going on."

"You wouldn't, Daddy," Carrie shrieked with delight.

"He certainly wouldn't," Carrie's mother answered for him. "Your father is kidding."

"Am I?" Mr. Macphail asked wickedly. "This suit is pretty loose on me. I'm sure I could find a place to hide these tests and sneak them in."

"Then I'll just have to frisk you before we go inside."

"Mom," Carrie said, interrupting their banter, "you didn't really answer me. How long am I going to have to stay at Luke's?"

"Carrie, just as long as it takes," Mrs. Macphail replied as she parked the car.

Carrie took a look around as she grabbed her peanut book and climbed out from the back seat. Luke's neighborhood was more modest than her own. The houses were smaller and not quite as nicely kept up. Still, there was a lovely pink rosebush blooming in front of the Olsons' house and the wooden window boxes were filled with cheery orange and yellow mums.

"Hey, how about a kiss?" Mr. Macphail called, rolling down his window. Carrie gave him a peck on the cheek and followed her mother up the wooden stairs. She waited a little nervously while Mrs. Macphail banged the brass knocker.

Mrs. Olson was older than her mother, but Carrie was surprised to see that she was very pretty. Her mother had told her that the Olsons were divorced, so it would be just Mrs. Olson going to the dinner with them.

"Carrie, we're so glad you're here," Mrs. Olson said pleasantly. Carrie looked around the plainly furnished room. There was no one else there. Whom did Mrs. Olson mean by "we"? Just then, Luke wandered in, his straight brown hair falling into his eyes and a book under his arm.

"Here's Carrie and Mrs. Macphail," his mother said in a hearty tone of voice.

"Oh hi," he answered absently. With hardly a glance in their direction, he sat down on the couch and opened his book.

Mrs. Olson frowned, but Luke was too busy reading to notice. "And, of course, I want you to meet Tammy." She called up the stairs and in a moment Tammy appeared. A tall, thin girl of fourteen or fifteen, Tammy looked about as pleased with this baby-sitting arrangement as Carrie. She politely said hello to Mrs. Macphail, but she barely gave Carrie a nod.

"Well, now that you're all acquainted, it's really time we get going," Mrs. Olson said, looking at the mantel clock.

There was a flurry of good-byes and then Carrie found herself alone with Luke and Tammy Olson. She was just wondering what to say when Tammy solved the problem for her.

"Carrie, I'm going to lay things on the line. My

boyfriend is coming over in about five minutes and I don't want to see you or Luke down here all evening. Got that?"

Carrie cast a sidelong glance in Luke's direction to see how he was taking this announcement, but he was still engrossed in his book. She decided she'd better stand up for her rights.

"I'm a guest," she said stubbornly. "I think I should be in the living room."

Tammy hooted. "You're not a guest. You're just a kid who's too young to stay by herself."

Carrie was instantly deflated. She couldn't argue with that.

"But you're not a baby," Tammy continued smoothly. "At least, I hope you're not. So you're perfectly capable of taking care of yourself tonight."

Boy, I hope my parents aren't paying you much, Carrie said to herself. "So where do you want me to be if not in here?" Carrie asked, a note of defiance creeping back into her voice.

"Luke's room."

Carrie looked at her with unbelieving eyes. "I don't want to stay in Luke's room."

At this, Luke finally looked up from his book. "Why not? I've got some really neat things we could look at."

"I just don't want to," she insisted stubbornly.

Luke shrugged and went back to his reading.

Before Carrie could say anything else, the doorbell rang and Tammy answered it. Giving Tammy a kiss was one of the biggest guys Carrie had ever seen. He wasn't just tall, he was wide and, not surprisingly, he was wearing a Forest Glen High School football jersey. He peered over Tammy's shoulder. "This the kid?" he inquired, none too politely.

"Yep, and she doesn't want to clear out. She wants to stay in here."

"Oh, is that so?" The hulk lumbered toward her. "What's your name, kid?"

"Carrie. What's yours?" she made herself ask.

"Joe. Now look, Carrie, me and Tammy were supposed to go out tonight till she got stuck with this baby-sitting thing. So we decided to stay home and watch TV. Alone. You don't want to ruin our night," Joe insisted. "Do you?"

Her night was already ruined. She might as well give in. "I guess not."

"Fine," Tammy said, seizing the advantage. "Luke, get going."

Joe snickered. "Yeah, buddy, show her that great room of yours. Tammy, do you think we can trust these two up there alone?"

"Creep," Carrie mumbled under her breath. She straightened up and tried to walk out of the room with some dignity. But as she moved toward the stairs, she realized she didn't exactly know where to find Luke's room.

"It's the first one on the right," Luke whispered, coming up behind her. She could hear Joe's giggle following them from the living room.

"Don't mind him," Luke said as they climbed the stairs. "His brain's too small for his body."

"That's for sure." Carrie couldn't have been more surprised to hear a civil remark coming out of her mouth. She clamped her lips together.

But even if she had been chattering away, Carrie would have been struck speechless when Luke opened the door to his room. A year or so ago the Macphails had driven out to the West Coast. In San Francisco they had gone to the zoo and one of the buildings was an insecterium that housed all sorts of weird and wonderful creepy crawlers. Luke Olson's room reminded Carrie of that insect zoo.

Everywhere she looked there were glass terrariums with bugs in them. Spiders, ants and beetles were just a few of the insects she saw as she glanced from dresser to desk to table. Carrie wasn't afraid of insects, but she couldn't imagine anyone living here, not even Luke. The room had an earthy smell that was coming either from the bugs or from the dirty clothes piled on a wooden chair.

Carrie looked at Luke. She expected he would be waiting for some comment, but instead he was busying himself with a few spiders in a glass jar. He seemed to have forgotten she was there. Carrie cleared her throat and finally Luke turned around. "You're not afraid of insects, are you?" he asked.

She shook her head no.

"That's good," Luke said matter-of-factly. "A lot of girls are. Some guys, too. Joe, for one," he said with a smile.

Carrie reacted with surprise to that smile. They had been together since the third grade and Carrie couldn't ever remember seeing Luke smile.

"Doesn't your mother mind all this?" Carrie asked, gesturing. She had forgotten she wasn't speaking to him.

"She feels sorry for us since my dad left."

"But even so," Carrie insisted.

"I'm very careful," Luke said seriously. "I make sure none of them get loose or anything." He paused. "Of course, I do have to clean the room. My mother won't come in here."

Carrie nodded. She could understand that.

"I'm going to feed some of them now."

That sounded pretty interesting, but Carrie didn't want to act as if she cared. She was still clutching her peanut book. "I'm going to read," she announced.

"Sure, if that's what you want," Luke said. "You can take my desk chair, or sit on the bed."

"I'd rather have the chair," she said, looking pointedly at the mound of dirty clothes.

It took Luke a second to catch on, then he got embarrassed. "Oh right." He gathered up the clothes and dumped them on the bed.

"Thank you," Carrie said coolly and sat on the straight-backed chair. There was no way to get comfortable, but Carrie didn't want to feel comfortable in Luke's room. She was just getting into George Washington Carver and his experiments with the peanut when she happened to look up and see a bottle of live flies in Luke's hand. Fascinated, she watched as he unscrewed the bottle cap and began feeding flies to some green insects in a big glass terrarium.

"Oh gross." The words slipped out of her mouth.

Luke turned around. "Uh?" he said absently.

"Are you feeding flies to those bugs?"

"Praying mantises," Luke corrected. "I have to. They're hungry."

"Can't you feed them something decent?"

"Like what?"

"Like lettuce."

"They don't like lettuce. They like flies."

Carrie shook her head and was trying to settle back into her book when she caught the movement

of something big and black out of the corner of her eye. She leaned across the desk to stare into the windowsill terrarium. A small scream caught in her throat. That was no ordinary spider in there, that was the biggest, hairiest spider Carrie had ever seen or ever dreamed of seeing. "Luke," she said in a strangled voice, "what is that?"

Luke walked over to the window. "It's a tarantula. Her name's Frieda."

Carrie sat back down on the chair. "Isn't she dangerous?"

"Not really. Tarantulas don't bite humans. At least, this kind doesn't."

"She's so big." Frieda was at least as big as Carrie's hand. Some people would think of stepping on a spider if they wanted it out of the way, but you couldn't step on Frieda. It would be like stepping on a mouse. "Where did you get her?" Carrie couldn't help asking.

"My mom knows someone at the hospital who goes insect collecting in Central America. He brought me Frieda about a year ago. Do you want to see her up close? I could take her out."

"That's all right," Carrie said hastily. "But you can take her out, really?"

"Sure. They can't be handled too much, of course."

Carrie got a dreamy look on her face. "Maybe we

could take Frieda to your sister's room and stick her in a drawer."

For the briefest of seconds, their eyes caught and another smile appeared on Luke's face. It turned into a chuckle. "I couldn't do that. Tammy's sticking her hand in those drawers all the time and she might frighten Frieda. My sister's pretty scary, in case you haven't noticed."

"I noticed." Carrie laughed and Luke joined her.

It seemed to Carrie as though some kind of invisible barrier had been lowered. And she had to admit that Luke's room, though weird, was pretty intriguing. "What else do you have in here?"

That was all the invitation Luke needed. In his deliberate way, he began in one corner of the room and showed Carrie all of his bugs. There was an ant farm that fortunately seemed pretty secure, a group of beetles crawling around in dirt and rocks and a butterfly collection pinned to a board, which Luke assured Carrie was bought in a junk store. He would never catch butterflies and kill them, but since these were already dead and pinned, well, they were interesting to look at.

"I bet you're going to have a wonderful science project," Carrie said enviously. Although she was making a valiant effort to find some special aspect of the peanut, none had grabbed her yet.

"I am," Luke agreed. "I think I should make it to the science fair."

Carrie admired the way Luke said that so confidently. Carrie knew in her heart that even if she could get Mr. Peanut to sing, dance or stand on his head, she had very little chance of being in the science fair. A dancing peanut wasn't very scientific. It just had pizzazz.

"What exactly are you doing for the project?" Carrie asked.

He motioned her over to one of the glass terrariums sitting on his dresser. It was almost empty, so Carrie could clearly see a caterpillar climbing up a twig. There was also a small shiny green- and buff-colored sac laying among the leaves.

"A caterpillar and a cocoon?" Carrie asked.

"A caterpillar and a chrysalis," he corrected. "But lots of people say cocoon. A few days ago, the chrysalis was a caterpillar and pretty soon it's going to turn into a cabbage butterfly."

"When?" Carrie asked with excitement. It would be really something to see that happen.

"According to my charts, in about ten days."

"And that's going to be your science project?"

"Yep, I'm going to hand in my notes." He dragged out a worn leather-bound notebook. Each page was dated and filled with Luke's observations about the state of his caterpillars and chrysalises. Luke's cursive writing wasn't very clear, and his jottings were messy, but Carrie was impressed nevertheless.

"That's neat."

"And if I get picked for the science fair, I'll display four or five caterpillars in various stages of their development, so people can see them. And I'll probably make a papier-mâché butterfly because it would really be mean to keep one in a glass case."

Carrie could see that Luke had thought this whole thing out. He looked happier than he had all night, even when he was smiling. "Well, you're going to be at the science fair. I mean, no one will have a project like yours."

"Oh, I don't know," Luke answered casually. "Miss Ryan is doing the picking, and she doesn't like me."

Carrie was surprised he could say that with such ease. She didn't know how to answer him. After all, it was true. Before Carrie could say anything, Luke spoke up again. "I don't like her much either."

Now Carrie was surprised all over again. Not like Miss Ryan? Before Carrie could digest this piece of information, Tammy appeared in the doorway.

"Joe had to go home," she said with disgust. "His brother's sick and his mother needed him to pick up some medicine. You can come downstairs if you want to." With that, she turned and stomped out of the room.

"Do you want to go down?" Luke asked politely.

Carrie thought it over. She could watch TV anytime, but how often did she get to look at tarantulas?

"No, let's stick around here," she said as casually as Luke had. "Show me some more bugs."

The next two hours flew by. Luke was good at explaining and told her a lot of interesting facts about insects. It was pretty clear that he really cared about his creatures. He didn't even mind the itchy bites he got when he went bug collecting. So that's why he has all those scabs, Carrie realized, looking at him with respect.

Most surprising of all was finding out that sober old Luke had a sense of humor. Of course, the insect jokes he was telling were pretty corny—*"You know where to buy bugs, Carrie? At a flea market!"*—but she had told some that were just as bad in her time.

When Carrie heard her mother's voice calling up the stairs, the thought that passed unbidden through her mind was, I don't want to leave. She found her peanut book under the bed where it had fallen and slowly straightened up. "Uh, thanks for showing me all this stuff."

Luke pushed his hand through his hair. "That's okay. See you Monday."

Luke's words sent a chill through Carrie. He would expect to talk to her on Monday, to be friendly. She pictured how the other kids would tease her if they caught her in a conversation with old Luke the Puke.

Suddenly she knew what she had to do, even if it made her a little ill.

"Luke, listen," Carrie began in a rush. "In school, well, I don't think it would be too good if you talked to me." She stopped, not knowing what else to say.

Luke looked at her steadily. "Yeah, I guess that wouldn't be too good."

"Well,bye." Carrie couldn't bear to be around him anymore. "I'm sorry," she added in a whisper as she left the room, but she wasn't sure that Luke had heard her.

"CHILDREN," MISS RYAN BEGAN as they got settled after returning from the art room, "I want to talk about our science projects, and then tell you about the big social studies assignment you'll be responsible for after your projects are turned in."

The class groaned, making Miss Ryan smile. "It's terrible, I know."

Carrie looked at her teacher with a shining face. In a long blue-jean skirt and a bright yellow turtleneck, Miss Ryan was a happy dab of color in an otherwise gray and rainy day. Her brown eyes sparkled as she looked around the room. "Your science projects are due in a few days, so let's take a few moments and you can tell me what you've been working on. How about you, Vicki?"

Vicki, a short mousy girl, answered proudly, "I'm identifying autumn leaves."

How original, thought Carrie.

"How many of you are working on a project about leaves?" Miss Ryan asked. About half the kids raised their hands. Miss Ryan gave a little sigh. "I see. What else is anyone working on?"

Carrie raised her hand, but Miss Ryan smiled and nodded at Randy.

"I'm studying avocado plants. I'm growing one from a seed."

"What a good idea, Randy. I'll look forward to hearing more about it."

Avocados, peanuts, they weren't all that different. Carrie toyed with her pencil. She hadn't even grown a peanut, she was just planning a chart. Slowly she lowered her hand.

"Yes, Luke, what about you?"

Before Luke could answer, several of the kids called out, "Bugs!" Freddy turned around in his seat and yelled, "He's bringing in some of his cooties!"

Miss Ryan automatically said, "Fred, none of that," but Carrie was almost sure she saw a twitch of a smile on her teacher's face. No, it couldn't have been, she thought. Not even Coach Grady would have laughed at a stupid remark like that.

"I am doing insects," Luke said without emotion. "I'm tracing the life cycle of the cabbage butterfly."

"Very interesting. Wendy?"

Carrie had a wild urge to get up and tell everyone just how interesting it was, but of course she couldn't. She hadn't so much as looked in Luke's direction since that night at his house, and true to his word, Luke hadn't said anything to her.

"Class, I'm glad to hear you're all getting on with your science projects," Miss Ryan said after listening to a few more students. "When you hand them in, I'll evaluate them and choose the ones to be entered in the science fair. I have been told our class will have two entries and from the sound of things I won't have an easy time picking them."

That, Carrie knew, was simply teacher talk. Most of the projects sounded hopelessly boring. Miss Ryan would be lucky if she could find another good entry besides Luke's.

"Now, on to social studies. As you're finishing up science, this will give you something to think about." Gracefully, Miss Ryan started walking around the room. "One of the most exciting things in the world is traveling. I have been all through France and West Germany, and those trips were some of the best times in my life."

Carrie gazed out the window at the empty playground. She wasn't surprised that Miss Ryan had done a lot of traveling. Traveling was something she wanted to do, too. So far, the farthest she had ever gone alone was to St. Louis to visit her grandmother. Sitting in her faded train seat watching the miles fly by had been fun, but Carrie was eager to have her first plane ride, or better yet, a ship voyage. She pictured herself gaily waving good-bye to her parents from the top deck, the way people did in those cruise commercials. Maybe Miss Ryan had some sort of trip planned for them. Carrie turned her attention back to what was being said.

"At the end of the week, each of you will choose a country you would like to know more about. You will have to go to the library and use other outside sources to learn about your country. Then you will prepare notebooks so you can share what you've learned with the rest of the class. That way, we'll feel like we've been on visits all over the world. So I want you to start thinking about which country you would like."

Carrie was disappointed. Notebooks were hardly exciting. As a matter of fact, the assignment sounded exactly like the reports they had done on the United States in the fourth grade. Carrie had wanted Vermont, but Michelle Mitchell asked for it first. Carrie had gotten stuck with her own state, Illinois. Who wanted to write about their own state?

While Miss Ryan went on speaking, Carrie decided that she really wanted to write about England.

Knowing Jane had made it seem like a real place and besides, England was so romantic, with its princes and princesses. Ideas for her notebook were forming in her mind when Carrie suddenly had an awful thought. What if Beth wanted England? After all, Jane was her *au pair*. By some invisible right, it seemed that England should belong to Beth.

Later that afternoon, Carrie brought up the subject with Beth. They were lounging around the Stones' family room, supposedly working on their science projects. With her mouth full of Jane's shortbread, Carrie asked outright, "Beth, are you choosing England for your social studies country?"

Beth was sitting cross-legged on the floor, looking through her leaves for about the tenth time. "Nope," she said without even looking up, "I'm picking Israel. My aunt lives there and we'll probably be visiting her next summer. If I do the report, I can start finding out about it now," she added practically.

Carrie's lips twitched into a smile of relief. "Then I'm going to take England."

"That's nice." Beth's attention was on a red and yellow leaf. She held it up. "What do you think of this one?"

Carrie gave it a critical look. "You've got better ones."

Beth took a sip of her milk and placed the glass on

a nearby coffee table. "You're right." She threw the leaf onto her fast-growing heap of discards. "How's the peanut chart coming?"

"Not great." Carrie looked down at the poster board she was working on. So far, all she had drawn was a big peanut with a face on it. Now she was trying to decide whether or not to add the top hat. The rest of the chart was going to explain how the nut started out as a flower on the peanut plant. When the flower fell off, the leftover part grew into a peg whose tip became the peanut. The *World Book Encyclopedia* had a nice chart that she was intending to copy.

Jane wandered into the family room with Sam toddling right behind her. "So, hard at work, are we?"

Beth picked up two leaves, an almost-black maple and a multicolored oak. "Which one do you like better, Jane?"

Jane settled into a white wicker chair and pulled Sam onto her lap. "You're driving us all barmy, Beth. Any of the leaves will do. Just get on with it and stick a bunch of them on the poster."

Beth bristled a little, but then her usual good nature took over. "You're right, I guess."

"Jane," Carrie began hesitantly, "I think I'm going to be doing a social studies report on England

and I was wondering if I could interview you for it."

"England, is it? Well, I do have a lot to say on that subject."

"Like what?" Carrie asked curiously.

"Americans seem to think the most important thing about England is Prince Charles and Princess Diana," she replied.

Carrie didn't say anything. She sort of thought that herself.

"But, in fact, there are some wonderful things and quite terrible things happening over there," Jane said seriously. "Sure, if you'd like to talk to me about it, I wouldn't mind."

"First, I have to make sure I get England as my country, but thanks, Jane, that would be great."

Sam, bored with being on Jane's lap, slid off, picked up some toys off the floor and began throwing them across the room. Then he burst into tears. Jane calmly walked over to the toddler and gathered him into her arms. "This young man wants to see his pillow, I'm afraid. Come on, then," she soothed Sam. "Let me know about the interview, Carrie," Jane called as she left the room.

Beth looked at Carrie with admiration. "What a good idea, talking to Jane. Your report will be great."

Before Carrie could answer, Michelle walked into the Stones' family room. Michelle's mother was friends with Mrs. Stone and Mrs. Macphail, so the three girls had known each other since the crib, practically. When they were three, they had all attended Kiddie Kollege Nursery School. Back then, Michelle was a crier who shrieked every time her mother left her there. Now all she did was whine, but she did that a lot. Carrie knew that if she met Michelle today they'd never be friends, but Michelle was like a habit that was too hard to break.

"Hi," Michelle said in her nasal voice. "What are you doing?"

"Science," Beth said briefly. "Sit down, Michelle." She was nicer to Michelle than Carrie was, but Carrie chalked that up to Beth's being basically a better person.

Michelle smoothed down the front of her tartan plaid skirt as she sat down. "Mine's already finished."

Carrie briefly caught Beth's eye. That figured. "You were doing birds, weren't you?"

"Yes," Michelle answered. "The life cycle of the robin."

"How come you finished so fast?" Beth asked curiously.

Michelle took a comb out of her pocket and ran it through her shiny black hair. She was very proud of that hair. "I didn't really have a choice. I had to finish it because Angelica was going out of town."

"Who's Angelica?" a puzzled Carrie asked.

"You remember," Michelle said. "She's the artist who works at my mom's advertising agency. She's drawing the grown-up robin and doing the lettering for my poster."

"That's not fair," Carrie said, shocked.

"I did all the rest of the work," Michelle answered. "I did all the research and drew everything else. Angelica's just doing some lettering and the robin."

"Still," Carrie insisted, "you shouldn't have somebody else draw on your poster."

"But I don't draw birds very well," Michelle said patiently as though she were talking to a three-year-old child, "and I wanted my poster to be really good."

There was no arguing with Michelle, Carrie decided. She looked down at her peanut. Maybe it wasn't that great, but it was all her own.

"Don't you think Miss Ryan will know?" Beth asked.

"Beth, it's not like this is a big secret or anything. It's just a little bird and some lettering. How many times do I have to tell you?"

Beth shrugged. "Hey, I don't care if you don't do it yourself."

"Did you see that sweater Miss Ryan was wearing today?" Michelle asked, changing the subject.

Beth put down her leaves. "Yeah, it was really beautiful."

"Don't you just love Miss Ryan?" Michelle said.

Carrie was taken aback by this turn in the conversation. She thought she was the only one who liked Miss Ryan in a very special way and she hadn't wanted anyone to know about those feelings. Now here was Michelle chattering away about Miss Ryan as though they were best friends or something. It didn't seem right.

"She's the best teacher we've ever had," Beth declared.

"That's not saying much," Carrie muttered.

"Don't you like her?" Michelle asked with surprise.

"She's okay," Carrie said. She didn't want anyone, especially Michelle, to see how she really felt.

"Oh, Carrie, you're just saying that because you think she doesn't like you," Beth said.

Carrie's head shot up and she glared at Beth. She had a lot of nerve spilling that secret after Carrie had confided in her. But one look at Beth's face told Carrie she wasn't saying it to be mean. Beth just didn't think it was any big deal.

"Come to think of it," Michelle said, twisting a strand of hair, "Miss Ryan doesn't like you much, does she?"

Carrie sat up stiffly. "I don't know what you mean. She likes me fine."

"But she never picks you for any of the special

jobs like feeding the fish," Michelle said thoughtfully.

"What's so important about the fish job?" Carrie asked crossly. "It's not exactly up there with being President of the United States, you know. Besides, I was class monitor just last week."

"That was because Miss Ryan was absent," Michelle reminded her. "The substitute picked you because she didn't know it was Randy's job, and he said that he didn't mind if you did it for one day."

Carrie glowered but Beth loyally put in, "Randy knew what a good job Carrie would do."

"Well, I'm just glad Miss Ryan likes me," Michelle said smugly. "She's so great, I just can't imagine how anyone wouldn't like her."

"I think Mr. Brown likes her," Beth giggled. "He's always hanging around when she has lunchroom duty."

"She wouldn't be interested in him. He's too . . . too . . . dopey," Carrie declared.

"Besides," Michelle added, "he teaches second grade."

"So what?" Carrie asked.

"If she teaches fifth-graders, her job is more important than his, so it wouldn't work out."

"Michelle, haven't you heard of women's liberation?" Beth asked. "Women can have more important jobs than men . . . if teaching fifth grade is more important than teaching second grade, which I'm not even sure of."

"I think it is," Michelle insisted. "But anyway, Carrie's right. Mr. Brown isn't nearly good enough for her."

When Michelle started agreeing with her, Carrie knew it was time to go home. "I think I'll work on my poster later," Carrie said, getting to her feet.

"You're doing peanuts or something, right?" Michelle asked. "Can I see it?"

"It's not really ready for anyone to look at yet."

Michelle, not one to take no for an answer, got off the couch and stepped over to the poster. "There's nothing on it," she declared.

Carrie glanced down at the poster lying on the floor. It was true. From this height, the peanut she had drawn so lightly was almost impossible to see. "Well, Michelle," Carrie said, picking up the posterboard, "that's because I drew it with invisible ink."

Michelle looked shocked. "Why would you do that?"

"Oh, it'll appear when Miss Ryan looks at it, but this is part of the project because I made the invisible ink out of peanut oil."

"You did not."

"Yes, I did. Actually, a friend of my mother's made the ink for me. He's a magician."

"That's not fair," Michelle said, pouting.

"But, Michelle, I just wanted my poster to be really good," Carrie said, quoting Michelle's own words back to her. She stole a look at Beth, who was choking back her laughter. "See you guys later."

CHAPTER

CARRIE CHECKED HER Mickey Mouse alarm clock and began dressing even faster. She had to bring her peanut poster to school today and she didn't want to be late.

She'd overslept because she had been up late putting on the finishing touches. And she had lost time this morning because she kept stopping every few minutes to admire her work.

I won't look again until I'm done dressing, she promised herself. She took her straight brown hair and pulled it back with a barrette. She slipped on her pink cotton turtleneck and topped it with a gray pullover. She dragged on her jeans. Then, while she was rummaging through her drawer for her gray socks, she caught sight of the poster leaning against her headboard and she just had to stop and look at it again.

It was really good. She had finally gotten the large peanut with the smiling face and the top hat just right and then she had drawn over the pencil lines with gold ink. He was just for fun, but Carrie felt Mr. Peanut was a great touch. The four-part chart showing how the peanut plant developed was just fine and even the lettering was very neat. Instead of leaving the poster on the floor where Taffy could have stepped on it in the night, Carrie had carefully put it in the closet where it was kept perfectly safe. There wasn't a spot anywhere on it, not even an erasure mark.

"Carrie," her mother called up from the bottom of the stairs. "You'd better hurry."

"I know."

"Did you hear me?" her mother said more loudly.

"Yes," Carrie yelled, "I hear you. I'll be right down." She grabbed the first pair of clean socks she could find and put on her Nikes without untying them. Carefully, she lifted the poster and walked downstairs. Her father was already gone and Mrs. Macphail was putting the breakfast dishes in the sink.

"Mom, I finished my peanut poster," Carrie said, placing it under the windowsill. She sat down to the milk and toast her mother had left for her.

"That's nice, sweetie," Mrs. Macphail said absently. "Oh, Carrie, will you tell your dad to load the dishwasher when you get home?"

"Sure. Do you want to see it?"

"Do I want to see what?"

"My poster."

Taking off her apron, Mrs. Macphail gave Carrie a kiss on the top of her head. "I'd love to, but I'm really running behind. Can't I see it later?"

"No." Carrie pouted. "I have to turn it in today."

"I wanted to see it last night, you know."

"But it wasn't done then."

"All right, let me have a look."

Before Carrie could grab the poster, the phone rang and Mrs. Macphail picked it up.

"Hello? Oh hi, Rita, what's up?" Her mother paused and began to look upset. "I'm sure Dr. Barger does want those blood samples now, but there's no way he can have them tested before eleven." Her mother listened again and pursed her lips together in a straight line. "All right, I'm leaving now. Start running the test and I'll be there just as soon as I can." She hung up the phone hard. "Ooh, that guy makes me crazy."

Carrie had heard tales of the bullying Dr. Barger before. "What's he doing now?"

"He wants some blood work done day before yesterday," her mother answered, pulling on her sweater. "Carrie, I'm really sorry, but I've got to get to the hospital right now. I promise we'll spend time looking at your poster when you get it back." She gave Carrie a swift kiss, grabbed her car keys and hurried out the door.

With a sigh, Carrie looked for the brown packing paper her mother had brought home yesterday. When she found it, along with scissors and Scotch tape, she carefully set the poster down and covered it with the paper. She was taking no chances that it might fall on the ground or get mussed up in any way.

Knowing that Beth must already be waiting on the corner, Carrie gathered up her things and, making sure the door was locked, rushed down the street.

"C'mon," Beth said as soon as she spotted Carrie. "We're going to be late."

"Sorry," Carrie said briefly. They walked quickly toward school. "Did your project come out okay?"

"I think so. I just hope these don't fall off." Beth hadn't covered her poster because she was afraid she'd crush the leaves.

"We're almost there," Carrie assured her and by running the last block they managed to slide into their seats before the last bell rang.

"Class, I see you all have your science projects with you, so let's get them out of your way. Row by row, I want you to come up and put your posters and models against the wall."

Miss Ryan looked pretty happy, Carrie noticed. The idea of looking at twenty-two different science projects wouldn't have made Carrie's day, but Miss Ryan seemed excited about the prospect as she directed the children to various places around the room.

Since Carrie was in the last row, she tried to get a good look at the other kids' projects as they carried them up, but all she managed was a glimpse here and there. She did notice that Michelle Mitchell's poster looked as though it had been illustrated by a professional artist and was a lot nicer than anyone else's. So what, Carrie sniffed to herself. It's easy to be good if an adult is helping you.

She also saw Luke bring up his battered old notebook. Miss Ryan gave him a funny look, but told him to put it down next to Peter Lennon's model of the solar system.

Then it was Carrie's turn. As her row stood, she pulled off the brown paper, threw it in the basket on the way up and placed the poster lovingly under a window where Miss Ryan pointed.

The morning continued smoothly enough. They selected their countries for the social studies unit and Carrie got England. She was surprised it had gone so easily and she flashed Beth a smile.

After they'd put their math books away, Miss Ryan said, "Class, I'm going to give you half an hour or so to read on your own while I sort these science projects out by subject. Take out your library books and begin to read quietly."

There was a great clatter as they all dug into their desks. Then the class settled down as people began reading. Since Carrie was a fast reader and almost done with her book, she decided to watch Miss Ryan's reactions to the various science projects. Slumping down in her seat and keeping her book up, she peered over the top of it as Miss Ryan divided the science projects into groups.

She couldn't see as much as she wanted to, but she recognized Beth's poster when Miss Ryan came to it. The teacher simply put it in the ever-growing "leaf poster" category without giving it a second glance. Carrie also recognized Freddy Butler's poster on electricity. Carrie had noticed it because Freddy sat just two rows away from her and because it wasn't very good. He had done it in tempera paints that looked as though they hadn't dried properly. They were all runny and caked around the edges of the posterboard. Miss Ryan put Fred's poster on the side by itself.

When Miss Ryan got to Michelle's poster, Carrie was annoyed to see the teacher smiling as she put it with the other animal projects. But before Carrie could fume, she saw that Miss Ryan was now looking at her own peanut poster. Was that a frown on Miss Ryan's face? Carrie's heart sank as she saw her poster go right next to Freddy Butler's.

For the rest of the period, Carrie worried. Why was her beautiful poster sitting next to Fred's caked-up hunk of junk?

When it was almost time for recess, Miss Ryan asked for the children's attention. "For the most part, I'm very pleased with what I saw here, class. I can tell you put a lot of effort into your projects. Luke, Fred and Carrie, I'd like to see for a few moments. The rest of you may line up for recess."

Now Carrie was completely confused. Luke's project had to be one of the best. She brightened. Maybe hers was one of the best, too. Confidently, she walked up to the front of the room while the rest of the kids looked on curiously.

"All right, class, quietly." Miss Ryan walked to the head of the line and led them outside.

"I didn't have time to do the stupid project," Freddy said angrily as soon as everyone was out of the room.

Luke didn't say anything, so Carrie felt it was up to her to put in a cheerful word. "She probably likes ours best."

Freddy glared at her and Luke turned his head

away. Carrie was about to tell Luke she already knew his project was good. Then she quickly remembered that she didn't want anyone to know she had spent time with him, least of all that bigmouth Freddy Butler. He'd blab it to everyone and she'd never live it down. She shut her mouth and stared down at her shoes.

In a moment Miss Ryan returned and closed the door behind her. She gazed at them, disappointed. "I'm sorry to say that you three have turned in projects that are not up to standard. I'm afraid you're going to have to do them over."

While Carrie's mind raced, trying to figure out what could possibly be bad about the peanut poster, Miss Ryan turned her attention to Freddy.

"Fred, this poster is just too messy to be acceptable." She held up the sad-looking cardboard. Letters crowded together at the edge of the poster where Freddy had run out of room and the botched-up colors and lines looked even worse close up than they had from far away.

"My mother's been working overtime," Freddy muttered.

"Pardon me?"

"My mom's been busy at work and I've been taking care of my little brother," he said, kicking a little at the leg of her desk.

"Well, I'm sorry to hear that," Miss Ryan said

briskly as she handed the poster back to him, "but I'm sure someone can watch your brother for an hour or two while you redo your poster. Your schoolwork is important, too. Luke," she continued, "I've looked through your notebook and your handwriting is so bad that I can barely read your notes. I gather you are doing the life cycle of the cabbage butterfly."

"Yes," he answered, picking a scab on his wrist.

"Don't pick, Luke. Tell me, why didn't you hand in something more visual? A butterfly would have looked very nice drawn on a chart."

"I guess, but I had too much information for just a chart. I've been keeping notes for a long time."

Miss Ryan looked down at the stained notebook distastefully. "I see."

"And if I got chosen for the science fair, I was going to bring in the chrysalises and a model of . . ." His voice faded as he noticed Miss Ryan losing interest. "Anyway, I thought you'd want to see this, because entomologists keep notebooks."

"Luke, you are not an entomologist, you are a fifth-grader," Miss Ryan replied. "However, since it seems to suit your scientific sensibilities better, I will let you turn in your notebook. Just make sure I can read it."

Carrie waited unhappily as Miss Ryan paused before she turned toward her. "Carrie, your poster would have been fine. Unfortunately, you spelled peanut wrong every time it appeared. How do you spell peanut?"

Carrie wondered if someone could actually die of embarrassment. She wracked her brain. What could be so hard about peanut? "P-E-N-U-T?" she asked.

"There is an *a* in peanut," Miss Ryan said with a sigh.

"Where?" a bewildered Carrie asked. "I mean, if you sound it out, like you told us to do with words . . ."

"Silent *a*. P-E-A-N-U-T. Surely you noticed that in your reading on the subject."

Carrie had not. Of course, she hadn't been looking for it. Why would she? It certainly had no business being there.

"Carrie, this is pure carelessness."

"I'm sorry," she said, winking back the tears. Carrie, careless, why did those two words have to sound so much alike?

"Just do it over, Carrie." Miss Ryan looked at her watch. "There's ten minutes more left in recess. I will be out in the hall. Why don't the three of you begin doing something about your projects now?"

As soon as Miss Ryan left the room, Freddy turned and gave Luke a little shove. "Get out of my way, Bugface." Luke went back to his desk while Freddy sat himself down in Miss Ryan's chair and started looking through her grade book.

Carrie shuffled dejectedly back to her seat, dragging her poster with her. She hated it now. That stupid Mr. Peanut grinning up at her and everywhere she looked the word PENUT. She glanced over at Luke, who was in his usual pose, staring out the window. Feeling her gaze, he turned to her and, making sure Freddy was not looking, gave her a small smile. Carrie tried to smile back, but she really felt like bursting into tears. She checked her pockets for a handkerchief or tissue, but she didn't find either one. She didn't want the kids to come back and see her crying, so she decided she'd better go to the bathroom for a while.

Without a backward glance at Luke or Freddy, Carrie left the room. She supposed she should ask Miss Ryan's permission and checked around to see if she was nearby. Was that her voice coming from Mrs. Price's room down the hall? Carrie headed that way. Before she got to the doorway, she heard Miss Ryan talking to Mrs. Price: ". . . with the word peanut spelled wrong about twenty times," she chuckled. "Peanut!"

Without waiting to hear another word, Carrie walked quickly away, her face blazing red. She would not cry, she told herself over and over again, but before she could reach the girls' bathroom, she burst into tears.

"IT'S REALLY MOM'S FAULT," Carrie yelled. "If she had looked at my poster instead of just going to her stupid job, she would have noticed."

Mr. Macphail ran his hand through his sparse hair and paced the living room floor. "Carrie, I understand that you feel terrible about this, but you can hardly blame Mom. It was your own responsibility to check the spelling."

Carrie knew this was true, but she wasn't about to admit it. Why shouldn't her parents share the blame? she thought bitterly. That's part of their job, to make sure their child doesn't make a fool of herself.

She certainly had felt like a fool in school. After a short, hard cry in the bathroom, she ran back to the room and shoved the poster in the cloakroom, just seconds before the kids filed in from recess. Carrie was praying no one would ask her about the poster and no one did. Still, she was sure that a couple of the kids were looking at her curiously, even though she had done a good job of washing away her tears with cold water.

At lunchtime, in answer to Michelle's question, Carrie had said her peanut poster contained a few spelling mistakes and then changed the subject by saying she had to go to the library. Instead, she'd sneaked back to the cloakroom, taken the poster to the big wastebasket in the janitor's closet and dumped it in. There were rough copies at home so she could do it over, but this poster she never wanted to see again.

All afternoon she had longed to be home. After school she had raced home without waiting for Beth and now she was in the living room, Taffy lapping at her cheek to make her feel better while she told her father what had happened. Well, not all that happened. She would never tell anyone what she overheard Miss Ryan say. Carrie buried that snatch of conversation deep inside her, as deep as a hole she once dug to bury a bird.

"You know," her father continued, "we gave you a dictionary so you could look things up."

"Why would I have looked it up?" Carrie said defiantly. "I thought I was spelling it right."

"Carrie, I think Miss Ryan is being more than

fair. She's not going to mark you down if you redo the poster, right?"

"Right," Carrie admitted.

"And except for the spelling, she said everything else was okay?"

"Yes."

"Well, speaking as a teacher, I think you are lucky to be getting a second chance." He sat down on the couch and held out his arms to her. "Come here, baby."

Carrie went to him and nestled in the safety of his hug. "I think you are more embarrassed than anything else," he said comfortingly.

The memory of Miss Ryan's voice as she laughed with Mrs. Price wafted like a breeze through Carrie's brain. "I guess so," she said.

"Just redo the poster and then next time try hard to do something Miss Ryan can really appreciate. Okay, pumpkin?" He rubbed his scratchy beard against her cheek.

"Okay," she answered. Her father was a teacher, so he was probably right. Her next project would be better. Miss Ryan had a right to laugh at her misspelling peanut. Who wouldn't?

Taffy started barking as the doorbell rang. Crawling out of her dad's lap, Carrie walked over to answer it. Beth was waiting outside.

"Where did you disappear to after school?" Beth

asked, bouncing in. "I turned around and you were gone."

"Oh, I just wanted to talk to my dad."

"Hello, Beth," Mr. Macphail greeted her as she followed Carrie into the living room. "What's doing?"

"Not too much. Carrie, do you still want to go to the library?"

They had talked about working on their social studies reports at the library early this morning. It seemed like ages ago to Carrie.

"I'll drive you over if you want," Mr. Macphail offered.

Carrie roused herself. "No, that's all right. We can walk." Anything was better than sitting around thinking about this terrible day.

The library was about half a mile away in the center of town. Looking at the store windows made it a pretty interesting walk.

"So you said at lunch you spelled some words wrong on your poster?" Beth asked idly as they were passing the Country Kitchen bakery.

"Uh-huh," Carrie said vaguely. She certainly didn't want Beth to know the "words" were peanut, over and over again.

Beth, who had a terrible sweet tooth, stopped to look in the bakery window. "I'm sure other kids misspelled words, too. It was just bad luck she noticed yours."

"Hey, do you want a chocolate chip cookie?" Carrie asked, trying to change the subject. She fished around in her jeans and pulled out two quarters. "We could split one."

"That would be great," Beth said, her attention diverted. But after they had purchased and carefully split the cookie and began heading again toward the library, Beth picked up the conversation where she left off.

"Did Luke and Freddy make spelling mistakes, too?"

"No, I think Miss Ryan said their projects were messy or something," Carrie said, trying hard not to be specific.

Beth giggled. "Did you see that old brown notebook Luke handed in?"

"It was full of really interesting stuff," Carrie said, bristling.

Beth looked at Carrie with surprise. "How do you know?" she asked.

"I saw it while Miss Ryan was taking you all out to recess," Carrie said, thinking quickly. "It was about caterpillars and butterflies."

"He should know about that subject. His house is probably crawling with all sorts of things, he's so bug crazy."

This was too close to the truth for Carrie. Luckily, Randy Jackson was just coming out of the drugstore and when Beth saw him, all thoughts of Luke Olson went out of her mind.

"Hi, Carrie. Hi, Beth," Randy said in his usual friendly way.

"Hi, Randy," Beth answered shyly. "How come you're downtown? I mean, aren't you going out for football?"

Randy fell in beside them. "No," he said, opening a pack of gum and offering it to the girls.

"Why not?" Carrie asked curiously. From what she had heard in the playground, it seemed as if going out for junior football was a big deal.

Randy shrugged. "I just don't like football that much. I told Coach Meier that a bunch of us wanted a soccer team, but he's all gung-ho about football."

"So you're not going to be in any after-school sports?" Beth wanted to know.

He shook his head. "I'll keep trying to get up a soccer team, for Saturdays, maybe."

"Can girls play, too?" Beth asked.

"Sure, if they want to."

Beth smiled. "I might want to try out."

Carrie gave her a skeptical look. Beth was not much more of an athlete than she was.

"You don't have to try out. Whoever wants to play can just come. I'll let you know if it gets organized."

"Great!"

"What about you, Carrie?" Randy turned to her. "I remember you kicked me pretty hard once in second grade. We could probably use you."

Normally Carrie would have teased him right back, but all she did was shake her head and say, "No, soccer's not for me."

"Oh okay." Randy gave her shoulder a friendly punch. "So where are you two going, anyway?"

"To the library," Beth answered. "Didn't you about die when Miss Ryan said we had to make oral reports instead of just handing in notebooks?"

That was a little bombshell Miss Ryan had dropped on them around three o'clock. She said that after thinking about it, she'd decided the class could kill two birds with one stone by giving their reports orally. This seemed like a terrible idea to everyone but Miss Ryan, who cheerfully told them speaking in front of each other would do them good. Now it looked as if at least one other person agreed with her. "I don't know," Randy was saying. "It might be fun."

Carrie marveled. If any other kid had said that, he would have sounded like a pompous jerk, but Randy's words, coupled with his sweet smile, made the whole thing sound reasonable. It appeared that Beth seemed to think so.

"Well, maybe you're right," she said, changing

her tune. "I guess we have to try new things."

"Sure," Randy said encouragingly.

He turned off at the next corner. The moment he was out of earshot Carrie said, "I don't think oral reports are a good idea. I think they're dumb. It's bad enough having to write the report, but who wants to listen to twenty-one more? They're all going to sound the same.

"Yours won't," Beth replied. "Not if you interview Jane."

"You might be right," Carrie said slowly. She could do something special, something that would redeem her in Miss Ryan's eyes.

"And Randy's will be good."

"Tell me the truth, Beth. You really like Randy, don't you?"

Beth nodded. "It's kind of embarrassing to talk about, but I do. He's nice, don't you think?"

"Yeah, he is." Carrie had to admit it.

"Do you think he likes me?"

The question bothered Carrie. What did she know about stuff like that? She was having enough trouble with peanuts. She didn't want to be bothered with boys.

By this time, they were at the stone steps of the library, a castle-like building covered with vines. "Maybe we'd better go in and get started, huh?" Carrie urged. "Most of the afternoon is gone already."

Beth followed Carrie into the lobby. "I guess I'll go into the children's room and start looking for books on Israel," she said unenthusiastically. "What about you?"

"I don't know yet. I want to think more about my report. I may not be using a lot of books. Right now, I'm just going to the adult department."

"Okay. Come find me when you're ready."

Carrie nodded and went into the quiet, sunny reading room. Every once in a while she found a book there she wanted to read, but mostly she came to get away from the little kids who ran around the children's area.

For a long while, she just thumbed through the books on England. Then she headed for the magazines and almost bumped right into Luke Olson, who was walking toward the door with a big book about butterflies under his arm. "Hi, Carrie," he said hesitantly.

Carrie looked over her shoulder. Beth was nowhere to be seen. "Hi, Luke," Carrie answered.

Luke shuffled from one foot to the other. "Have you started to do your peanut chart over yet?" he asked.

"Tonight," she said shortly. "What about you?"

"Oh, I'll try to get it done in a day or two. I've got a lot to copy over."

Carrie nodded. There was no doubt that their awful experience that morning had forged a bond between them. There was an awkward, short silence, then Carrie asked, "How's that chrysalis I saw at your house? Has it turned into a butterfly yet?"

"It ought to sometime today, if my observations are right. Nothing was happening, so I came to pick up this book. Otherwise, I'd be home watching."

"It must be neat to see."

"Do you want to come over tonight?" Luke asked. "It could happen then."

Carrie's face registered shock. How could she just go over to Luke's house as though he were a regular person?

Luke saw that she was startled. "I wouldn't tell anybody, if that's what you're worried about."

That remark made Carrie feel small, but she was glad Luke had said it. "I'm not sure I can come," Carrie said carefully, "but I'd . . . I'd like to." The moment the words were out of her mouth, she realized they were true.

Before she could say more, Carrie caught sight of Beth out of the corner of her eye, checking out her books at the circulation desk. "I've got to go," she said hurriedly. "Maybe I'll see you later."

"Uh, right." Quickly, Luke slipped away into the stacks.

CHAPTER

SOMETIMES CARRIE FELT BAD about how easy it was to make her mother feel guilty. Mrs. Macphail was broiling fish when she got home and almost burned it in an effort to pay some attention to Carrie.

"Hi, honey," she said when Carrie came through the kitchen door. "Daddy told me about your poster. I'm so sorry I didn't have a chance to look at it this morning."

Carrie shrugged and submitted to her mother's kiss. "Even if I'd showed it to you, I wouldn't have had time to fix it."

"But you could have turned it in late. I feel just terrible."

Good, was Carrie's immediate thought. Then she looked at her mother's tired face and she felt terrible. "It's not your fault, Mommy." Carrie thought it was babyish to say Mommy, but sometimes it just slipped out.

"Well, we both have to try harder. You to check your spelling and me to check you check your spelling. Oh, the fish!"

Carrie wrinkled her nose. Fish that wasn't burning smelled bad enough. Maybe this dinner would be too far gone to eat and they could go to McDonald's.

"Oh good. I got it just in time," Mrs. Macphail said. "Carrie, will you start setting the table?"

"Mom," Carrie asked as she put out the pretty pink and white china plates, "do you think I could go over to Luke's house tonight?"

Mrs. Macphail actually stopped in her tracks. "Luke Olson? I thought you hated Luke Olson."

Carrie didn't meet her mother's eyes. "I still don't exactly like him," she said, "but he's got a chrysalis at his house that's about to turn into a butterfly and I'd kind of like to see that."

"It's a school night, Carrie."

"I know, but it would be educational," Carrie argued.

"Tell you what. We'll call Luke after dinner and if the chrysalis is still a chrysalis, you can go over for an hour or so. But no longer. All right?"

"Thanks." Now that Carrie had gotten her own

way, she wasn't quite sure how she felt about it.

"I know Candy will be glad if Luke has a visitor. She says he doesn't have too many friends."

"He doesn't have any," Carrie replied shortly.

"But why not?" Mrs. Macphail said in that way parents have when they can't figure out why one kid in the class is unpopular.

"Because he picks his scabs and he's crazy about insects."

"Oh," said Mrs. Macphail, taken aback. "Oh."

"Come in," Luke called in answer to Carrie's knock.

"Hi," Carrie said shyly, but Luke hardly glanced in her direction. He was standing in front of an enclosed terrarium on his desk. From the doorway where she stood, Carrie could see the good-sized green ball inside.

Luke motioned her over. "See the way it's starting to wriggle around? That means it's going to be shedding its chrysalis soon. You got here just in time."

"That's great," Carrie whispered.

"You don't have to whisper," Luke said. "It can't hear you."

"I know that," Carrie said a little disgustedly, "but it seems like we should be quiet and have a little respect."

Luke looked at her with an expression akin to admiration. "You're right. We should show some respect."

Pleased, Carrie turned her attention to the terrarium. Luke pointed to the chair. "Why don't you sit down?" So Carrie pulled the chair up close to the desk. For what seemed the longest time, the chrysalis just wriggled about.

"I thought you said it was going to happen," Carrie said.

"It will."

"Are you taking notes for your project?"

Luke held up a pencil. "Yep, I wrote down when the movement started and I keep marking the time."

"I'm sorry about your having to do the notebook over," Carrie said, never taking her eyes off the terrarium.

"She didn't understand."

"Miss Ryan? Didn't understand what?"

Luke considered. "She didn't understand anything. Why it's important to keep a notebook instead of making just a poster, for one thing. And she doesn't understand about real science, that it's different than just collecting a bunch of leaves."

Carrie didn't know what to say. "You mean you think she's a bad teacher?"

For a long time there was silence. Finally he said,

"She's an okay teacher for most of the kids. But she's not for everybody."

Before Carrie could answer, Luke nudged her. "Watch, now, watch."

Carrie kept her eyes on the rolling chrysalis. Slowly a black head the size of a pin began to emerge. With the tiniest of movements, the heavy green skin moved and cracked until it was shucked off altogether. The chrysalis, now just an empty shell, was on the terrarium floor. And a damp butterfly, its wings plastered to its sides, trembled alone.

"Is it all right?" Carrie whispered.

"Sure. It'll take a few more hours until it dries and starts looking like a butterfly."

"Then you're going to let it go?"

"Yes."

"I wish I could be here for that."

Her words were interrupted by a knock on the door. Tammy stood there sourly. "Your mother says it's time to go home."

Carrie cast a longing look at the butterfly.

"Should I tell her you're coming?" Tammy asked impatiently.

"I guess so," she said, her eyes still on the terrarium.

Tammy followed her gaze. "Oh, another butterfly hatched? Don't worry, you can see that happen

around here anytime. We eat, sleep and drink insects around here, in case you haven't heard." With that, she slammed the door after her.

"Doesn't she make you mad?" Carrie burst out.

"Sure, but there are some things you can't really change."

"So what do you do about them?"

"I guess I just try and ignore them. Getting mad's usually not worth it."

"Is that why you never fight back against Freddy Butler?" Carrie asked thoughtfully.

"Definitely not worth it. Say, that reminds me of a joke. What kind of insects do knights fight?"

A smile played around Carrie's lips. "I don't know."

"Dragonflies!"

"Oh, Luke," she groaned.

"I made that one up. I'm starting to write jokes."

Carrie just shook her head. "I've got to go. Thanks for inviting me."

"You sound like you're leaving a birthday party," Luke laughed.

Carrie took one more look at the butterfly. "Well, in a way, I am."

CHAPTER

IT WAS LUNCHTIME before Carrie had a chance to say anything to Luke. She had handed in her poster first thing in the morning after working on it steadily from the moment she came home from Luke's until she went to bed. It hadn't taken as long this time around because she had left off the smiling Mr. Peanut. Now the chart was simply an explanation of the peanut's life cycle—crisp, clean, with the word peanut spelled correctly every time. She had checked it, her father had gone over it before she went to sleep and her mother looked at it again first thing in the morning. The funny part was, Carrie didn't really care about it anymore. She just wanted to get it turned in.

Miss Ryan had given the poster a cursory glance when Carrie brought it up to her desk. She didn't seem to notice that Mr. Peanut was gone. "That was quickly redone, Carrie," Miss Ryan had commented. "I'm happy to see you taking your work seriously. Just try to be more careful in the future. Next time I'll have to mark you down."

Carrie nodded yes and mumbled something about trying harder. She hurried to her seat with a great sense of relief.

The rest of the morning had been filled with the usual math and English lessons. Carrie looked for a private moment to ask Luke if the butterfly had gotten off all right, but there were always too many people around.

Now lunch was almost over and most of the kids had gone out to the playground. Carrie could see Luke sitting off by himself in the corner of the lunchroom.

"Do you want to go outside?" Beth asked, stuffing her leftover tuna sandwich in a brown paper bag.

Michelle wiped off her lip with a pink- and white-checked paper napkin. She glanced over at the window. "It looks like it might rain."

"So? We can come in if it starts raining," Beth said.

"Yes, let's go," Carrie said enthusiastically, "but I have to stop at the bathroom first. Why don't you two meet me outside?"

"We'll wait," Beth said.

"No, I'll find you."

"If we're going, let's go," Michelle said, pushing back her chair.

Carrie figured she could count on Michelle not wanting to wait around for her.

"All right," Beth said, standing up, too. "We'll be sitting on the steps, Carrie."

Carrie watched them walk out the door and hurried over to Luke. "Did everything go all right after I left?"

Luke rubbed his ear. "Oh sure. It dried and spread its wings. That took about an hour and a half and then I got out of bed around ten-thirty and let it out the window."

Carrie smiled. "What color was it?"

"White. I thought you knew. Cabbage butterflies are always white."

"I wish I could have seen it."

"Well, that was one thing Tammy was right about. I usually have some kind of butterfly or moth going through metamorphosis. You'll have another chance to see one go." He looked embarrassed. "That is, if you want to."

"I do want to," Carrie said, not embarrassed at all. Then she heard Michelle's unmistakable voice. "Carrie, what are you doing here?"

Carrie whirled around and saw Michelle and Beth standing right behind her. "I thought you were outside," she said stupidly.

"It started to rain," Beth answered.

Carrie looked out the window. Sure enough, large drops were splashing against the dirty panes.

Luke got up and gathered his books together. "I was just asking Carrie what page the math homework was on." Without a backward glance at any of them, he turned and walked away.

"Ugh," said Michelle, following him with her eyes. "What a nerd."

Carrie kept silent. "It's almost time to go," Beth remarked, looking at her watch.

The girls moved toward the front of the cafeteria. "He's not that bad," Carrie suddenly said, her voice testing out the words.

"Who?" Beth asked, puzzled.

"Luke."

Naturally Michelle hooted. "Luke? Carrie has a crush on Luke!"

"I do not," Carrie said wearily, having known something like that was coming. "But he's not that bad." Before any of them could say more, the bell rang and they filed into the hallway, back toward their classroom.

After school, Carrie and Beth headed toward the Stones' house. This was the day Carrie had arranged to interview Jane about England and she was getting excited about it. She had decided that she was going to make her report completely different from anyone else's. Instead of just a bunch of facts, she was going to have an eyewitness account of life in another country.

Carrie was also anxious to get to the Stones' so she could avoid any questions Beth might have about Luke. Michelle seemed to have forgotten about him—at least, she hadn't made any more cracks—and Carrie was hoping Beth would just let the whole thing pass, too. But they were hardly out of the schoolyard when Beth abruptly brought the subject up again.

"Carrie, did you really mean what you said?"

"About what?"

"That Luke's not that bad."

Carrie hesitated. "Yes."

"But you don't even know him," Beth said, confused.

Torn, Carrie didn't say anything at first. Then she got angry. "Actually, I've been to Luke's house twice."

"You have? Why?"

"The first time because I had to and the second time because I wanted to." Then she told Beth the whole story.

"I don't believe this. Why didn't you tell me before?" Beth asked, her upset plain.

Carrie was prepared for this question. "You don't tell me everything," she countered. "What about Randy? You never said you liked him until I asked you."

"Carrie, it's not the same. It was hard to talk about Randy."

"Well, it isn't exactly easy to talk about this."

Beth looked at Carrie with troubled eyes. "It all sounds neat about the butterfly and everything, Car, but are you really going to be friends with him?"

"Would it make any difference to you?"

"Not to me," Beth said a little too quickly, "but you know a lot of kids would laugh."

Carrie wanted to say, "So let them," but she couldn't, quite. Instead, she said nothing.

"So what are you going to do?"

"I don't know. Quit asking me," Carrie said crossly.

Beth looked hurt, but before Carrie could apologize, they arrived at the Stones', where Jane was waiting with tea and shortbread. Carrie noticed the maroon streak in her hair had been replaced with a gold one. It looked pretty nice.

"Your mum's taken Sam to the doctor for a checkup, Beth. Do you want to join Carrie and me for our talk?"

Beth grabbed a napkin and put a few pieces of

shortbread on it. "No. I'm going upstairs." She turned to leave the room, but Carrie pulled her aside. "I'm sorry," she whispered, "I just don't want to think about Luke any more today."

"You may not want to think about him, but you should. You're going to have to decide what to do about Luke," Beth said.

Carrie watched Beth climb the stairs until Jane's voice broke into her thoughts. "Let's get to it, then," Jane said, settling down on the family room couch.

Carrie took the swivel chair and pushed all thoughts of Luke and Beth out of her mind. "See, Jane, I want to really know what another country is like. The other kids are just going to get up and talk about a bunch of boring things like the minerals and the rainfall. Who cares?"

"No one, probably."

"Right."

"Your report is going to be different."

"I hope so. I want to find out things I can't get from library books."

"I think I see what you're getting at. Bird's-eye view and all that."

"That's it," Carrie said, her enthusiasm building.

"Well, it should work, then, seeing as how I'm a bird."

"A bird?"

Jane laughed. "A bird. It's British slang for a girl. Sorry, I like making up jokes."

Carrie thought about Luke, who also liked making up jokes. Then she reminded herself she wasn't going to think about him any more. She fished around in her knapsack for her notebook and pencil. "Okay, where do we start?"

For almost an hour, Jane talked and Carrie took notes. Every once in a while she would interrupt and ask a question, but mostly she listened.

"Carrie, we have to stop now," Jane said, looking at her watch. "I've got to get to my art class."

Carrie scrambled out of her chair. "Jane, thanks. This stuff is really great. I never thought about any of these things. I mean, like not knowing if you could find a job when you get out of school."

"You know, Carrie, I'm not the last word on any of this stuff. You are going to do some research, aren't you?"

"Sure, I've got plenty of books at home, but I wanted the personal touch, too. None of the other kids are going to have anything like this," Carrie gloated.

Jane swept shortbread crumbs off the table onto a saucer. "I hope you get a good mark, luv," she said.

Carrie smiled. "It's in the bag."

CARRIE STOOD IN THE SCHOOLYARD with Wendy, Michelle and Beth. The day before, Miss Ryan had read off the names of those who were giving their reports today, among them Carrie. So far, the class had heard ten reports and they were just as boring as Carrie had predicted. Now it was her turn and she couldn't wait.

"Oh look, Luke's back," Wendy commented as Luke walked past them. "I hope his chicken pox aren't catching any more."

"They wouldn't let him back in school if they were," Beth said.

Michelle gave a silly laugh. "He must have loved the chicken pox. More scabs for him to scratch."

"I wonder why he does that," Wendy said.

"Ask Carrie." Michelle giggled.

"Why would Carrie know?"

"She wouldn't," Beth said firmly.

Carrie wasn't sure if she should be grateful to Beth for answering or mad at her for butting in. She decided to ignore the whole thing. "Let's go inside," she said. "I want to look over the notes for my report."

The girls, along with some other fifth-graders, began straggling in at the sound of the first bell. Wendy and Michelle decided to stop at the girls' bathroom, so Carrie and Beth headed to their classroom. A few children, including Luke, were already at their desks. Miss Ryan was there, too, hanging up posters around the room.

"Hello, girls." She smiled as they came in. That grin pleased Carrie. "I'm hanging some of these posters for open house. I finally got them all graded. Beth, when you get your coat hung up, maybe you could give me a hand."

Carrie shuffled to her seat and threw her sweater over the back of her chair. Of course, Beth was taller than she was, Carrie told herself. Still, seeing Beth and Miss Ryan laughing as they hung up the posters gave Carrie a chilly feeling around her heart. She turned to see if anyone else was noticing what a good time Beth and Miss Ryan seemed to be having. There was plenty of hubbub in class as the kids started streaming in, but it was really only Michelle who looked enviously in Miss Ryan's direction as she put her books on her desk.

While Carrie was waiting for the second bell to ring, she glanced over at Luke, who was reading a book filled with glossy pictures of ants. Michelle had been blessedly silent about Luke, probably because he was home sick for more than a week. With Michelle it was out of sight, out of mind. Mrs. Macphail had told Carrie about Luke's mild case of the chicken pox and she even wondered if Carrie wanted to visit him. Carrie hadn't gone to visit, but she did find a riddle book with plenty of insect jokes at the school library. It was in her desk and Carrie wished she could give it to Luke right now.

The tinny ring of the final bell brought most of the kids to their seats. Miss Ryan waited until the room was quiet. "Good morning, everyone. As you can see, Beth and I were just putting some of your posters around the room, and before lunch I'll tell you who I've picked for the science fair. Now, however, I think it would be a good idea to start our social studies reports while we're still fresh and ready to listen."

Carrie wasn't sure her class was ever fresh enough to listen to oral reports, but she was certainly ready to get up and give hers. She listened as Miss Ryan called off the names of those who were to have their turns today.

"Let's see, Wendy, Marie, Freddy, Frank—oh, Frank's not here today—and Carrie. Would one of you like to go first?"

Carrie enthusiastically raised her hand, but Miss Ryan called on Freddy.

Freddy always seemed very confident when he was tripping kids or giving them the odd punch, but even though he swaggered to the front of the room, it was easy to see that public speaking made him nervous. His smile was sickly and he tapped his shoe lightly on the floor. "Australia," he began, clearing his throat. "Australia is a country and a continent."

Carrie figured that since Australia was a country and a continent, Freddy's report would be pretty long. Instead, after a few sentences about the country's location, its cities, frontier lands and "the funny-looking animals like the kangaroo," as Freddy put it, he promptly sat down.

Miss Ryan pursed her lips. "That was certainly short and to the point, Freddy."

"You told us not to read it," he replied. Miss Ryan had given specific instructions that the reports had to be spoken, not read, though note cards could be used.

"There wasn't much to read," Miss Ryan said dryly. She made a mark in her book. "Who's next?"

Carrie waved her hand. This would be a perfect time to give her report. She was sure to look even better if she followed Freddy. But Miss Ryan did not look in her direction and called on Wendy instead.

If Freddy was nervous, Wendy was the picture of confidence. "Spain, land of romance," she began.

Wendy may have considered Spain romantic, but that wasn't the impression that was coming across. She described the country's location, climate and mineral resources. She rattled off lists of statistics, everything from how many cows to how many indoor toilets the country had. Carrie looked around the room. People were passing notes and playing with their pencils. Michelle was Wendy's best friend, but even her eyes were glazed over. Eric Matten had given up entirely; his head was down in his arms.

But when Wendy finished, Miss Ryan gave her a big smile and said, "Wendy, when I assigned these reports, yours is exactly what I had in mind."

For the first time since she had interviewed Jane, Carrie felt some doubts. She turned around and looked at Miss Ryan, who was sitting at the back of the room. Did she really like that endless report? It certainly seemed as though she did. Carrie was sure the grade she was putting in her book was a big fat A. Before Carrie had more time to worry, Miss Ryan called on her. "Carrie, why don't you go up and tell us about England?"

Carrie made sure her shirt was tucked into her jeans as she walked up to the front of the class. She faced them and in a clear voice said, "Imagine your schooling is finished at age sixteen. If you didn't pass some very hard tests, you would not be able to go to college. But there aren't very many jobs for you either. What would you do?"

Although she tried to keep her eyes plastered to a back wall when she wasn't checking her note cards, Carrie could see that everyone was paying attention. At least, none of the kids had their heads down on their desks. Carrie went on to talk about some of the things she and Jane had discussed. About how hopeless young people felt when they didn't know when—or if—they would ever get work. She talked about how the British system of government was different from the American one and how it felt for a British person to come to the United States, a big country, very different from his or her own. She finished by saying, "Sometimes because both America and England speak the English language, people think they are like one country, but they are not. As you can see, they are very different."

Carrie looked at Miss Ryan. There was no smile

as there had been for Wendy, only a puzzled look.

"Carrie," Miss Ryan said slowly, "where did you get all that information?"

"I talked to an English person and I read a lot."

"I see. And you chose not to put in facts like the products of the country and the climate?"

Carrie could feel an angry little bubble growing in her stomach. "That's right. I thought the things I talked about were more interesting."

Miss Ryan looked as though she were groping for the right words. "Of course, it was interesting, Carrie, but I'm not sure fifth-graders have to be concerned about things such as British people not finding jobs. I wanted these reports to be a pleasant introduction to countries we might visit someday."

Carrie stood there, her face growing hot. She didn't know what to say.

"Now I can tell that you put lots of time into this," Miss Ryan said, "and it was different." She paused while Carrie thought, Different? She makes "different" sound like dogmeat.

"So," Miss Ryan continued brightly, "if you will just write a page or two showing you do know all the important facts about England, we'll consider this a complete report. Thank you. Marie, will you come up and tell us about Japan?"

As she walked back to her desk, a million thoughts

raced back and forth through Carrie's mind: the way the kids had paid attention to her report when they hadn't to the others. The way she had thought up the whole interview with Jane because she knew it would be different. How it turned out that Miss Ryan hated "different."

With Marie's voice droning in the background, Carrie forced herself to sort out her feelings. Surprisingly, she didn't feel ashamed. She knew her report was good. What she felt was mad. And she was upset because all of a sudden Miss Ryan seemed so . . . *dumb* was the only word she could think of. She glanced back over her shoulder to see how Miss Ryan was responding to Marie's unexceptional report on the wonders of Japan. She seemed to be liking it just fine.

The angry bubble in her stomach was blowing up, larger and larger. Then her thoughts were interrupted by Miss Ryan at the front of the room. "I think that's it for today's social studies reports. It's almost time for recess, but before I let you go, I want to tell you who will be going to the science fair." Carrie glanced over at Luke and sent him a small smile.

"Some of your posters and models were not the sort of things that could be expanded into science fair entries, and as I told you at the beginning of the semester, that was all right. For instance, Michelle Mitchell's lovely chart on the robin really doesn't lend itself to expansion, but we can all enjoy it anyway." Miss Ryan smiled at Michelle, who looked modestly down at her hands.

"However, I found two projects that I think would represent us well in the science fair: Peter Lennon's papier-mâché model that shows how the planets orbit and Randy Jackson's introduction to the avocado plant. Let's give them a round of applause."

While the other kids clapped dutifully, Carrie raised her hand. It was almost as if an unseen force were lifting it for her.

"Yes, Carrie?" said Miss Ryan, calling on her.

"What about Luke?" she asked, her voice quivering.

All heads turned toward Carrie. "I don't understand," the teacher said.

"He has caterpillars that turn into butterflies."

"Yes," Miss Ryan said coldly.

Carrie's eyes darted around the room. Beth looked positively pale and Luke's head was lowered as he nervously rubbed his thumb. "His project would have been great. He was going to bring in real caterpillars and cocoons—I mean chrysalises—that's the proper term—and people could see how they turned into butterflies. I saw it happen and it's the best scientific thing I've ever seen. It's practically a miracle."

Miss Ryan just stood there looking at Carrie. "I've chosen my two entries for the science fair."

Carrie never knew what possessed her, but she said in a very loud voice, "Maybe we could have a third. Since we have three good ones."

The silence in the room felt heavy. Finally Miss Ryan spoke in a light, bright voice. "I think that's against the rules, Carrie, but I'll certainly check and find out. And if Luke's caterpillars can't be in the science fair, perhaps he would bring them to school and we could enjoy them. All right, children," she said hurriedly, "let's line up for recess."

Carrie knew the whispers in line were about her, and as soon as the fifth grade got outside, kids came swarming up.

"Carrie, I can't believe you did that," Wendy said.

"When were you ever at Luke's house? You were kidding, right?" Michelle broke in.

"Nope, I was there," Carrie said cheerfully. The bubble inside her had burst and she felt surprisingly good. But her happiness faded when she realized the laughter she was hearing was directed at her.

She caught the words "Luke the Puke" from where Martin and Peter stood giggling together, and then Freddy's unmistakable voice calling her a hairy caterpillar. In front of her, two girls she barely knew whispered behind their hands. Carrie was now encircled, with most of the kids standing around in small knots, staring at her as though she were a bug in one of Luke's glass jars. Beth was at the very edge of the ring, her eyes down on the ground.

Now Freddy spoke to her directly. "Hey, Carrie, I've got a neighbor with a kitchen full of roaches. Do you want me to bring some in?"

"Why don't you shut up!" Carrie said furiously, but her voice was barely audible over the shrieks.

"Yeah," Martin piped up, "next time your family goes on vacation, maybe you can stay at a roach motel and visit some of your friends."

"Don't forget to keep your electric lights on, so you can attract plenty of moths," another voice yelled.

"You're a bunch of idiots, you know that?" Carrie shouted right back. "You're probably all too dumb to appreciate something like a caterpillar turning into a butterfly."

"I'd like to see that."

Carrie, winking back a tear, turned to see who had spoken.

"I think it sounds real interesting," Randy said.

"You do?" Carrie asked stupidly.

"Yeah. It's got to be better than watching an avocado plant grow."

There were chuckles at Randy's comment. Then Beth spoke up. "You're right, Randy. It would be great to see something like that. Carrie, you should really tell Luke to bring his stuff in." She stared at the other kids defiantly.

"Absolutely," said Randy, heading off toward a kickball game. "It sounds great."

A few of the kids nodded in agreement. When it looked like nothing else was going to happen, the group began drifting apart, singly and in pairs. Even Freddy—after one more crack about Carrie catching Luke's cooties—ran off to join the game.

Finally Carrie was left standing alone with Beth, Wendy and Michelle. Even though it was hot for autumn, Carrie felt cold from the inside out. She rubbed her hands up and down her arms. "So, I suppose you all think I'm crazy, right?" she said in a shaky voice.

Wendy touched her arm. "I think you're brave," she said quietly.

Beth's clear blue eyes looked straight into Carrie's gray ones. "I wish I was as brave as you."

"I don't know," Michelle said, tossing her hair over her shoulder. "Maybe everyone will forget about this, but honestly, you could have ruined your whole reputation, Carrie." She gave a small shudder. "I mean, Luke, ugh."

For some reason, Michelle, acting so perfectly like herself, made Carrie break into a smile. "I know, Michelle, it's weird, but as long as you stick by me, I'll be okay. Has anybody seen Luke, by the way?"

Michelle moaned. "Oh, Carrie."

"He's over there," Beth said, pointing to a corner of the schoolyard.

Carrie headed over to a deserted part of the yard where Luke sat on a stone bench reading the butterfly book she had seen him with at the library. He gave her a dazzling smile when she sat down.

"I have a joke," he greeted her.

"Let's hear it."

"Why is Carrie like an annoying mosquito?"

"I don't know. Why?"

"Because she bugs Miss Ryan."

Carrie laughed hard until she laughed away all the bad feeling. "It wasn't that funny, you know," she finally said.

"I know."

"I think I bug some other people, too."

"They've been giving you a hard time." It was a statement rather than a question.

Carrie shrugged. "It was just my day to open my big mouth, I guess."

"You sure did," he said admiringly.

"Are you going to bring your caterpillars to school?"

"Do you think I should?"

"Yes, I do. Some people, like Randy, already said they wanted to see them."

"I guess I could," Luke said thoughtfully. Just then, a speck of white flitted in front of them. "Look, Carrie." Luke pointed. "There's a cabbage butterfly."

Carrie watched intently as it balanced delicately on a twig for an instant before flying away. Then she turned to Luke with shining eyes. "Do you think it could have been ours?"

Luke smiled. "You never know, Carrie. You just never know."